YOUNGEST

SIGNS OF THE PROPHECY BOOK ONE

DEBBIE MUMFORD

WDM
Publishing

The Saga Begins...

Gwen Vaughan pushed her linguistic textbooks away and stood, stretching the cramped muscles in her lower back. Tucking a loose strand of shoulder length dark hair behind her ear, she glanced around the apartment she shared with Emily Stevens.

The two girls had gravitated to each other during their first day's orientation at the University of Colorado's Boulder campus and had been friends ever since. It's possible their friendship was an "opposites attract" kind of thing — gregarious, fun-loving Emily was about as different from studious, dependable Gwen as you could get — but whatever the reason, they'd remained friends through their undergraduate years.

Today was a perfect example of the differences in their psyches. It was her twenty-second birthday (and a mere three days before Christmas!), and where was Gwen? Out partying with friends? Home on the ranch with Aunt Katie and Uncle Jem?

Nope.

In her apartment. Alone. Studying.

Sighing and shaking her head, Gwen ambled to the kitchen to brew a pot of cinnamon tea and scrounge a blueberry muffin, but she stopped after only a few paces.

Something wasn't right.

SIGNS OF THE PROPHECY SERIES:

- Youngest
- Seeker
- Chosen

COPYRIGHT

PRAISE FOR DEBBIE MUMFORD

Praise for *Sorcha's Heart*

Katie from Goodreads: Five stars: 'This story was fantastic...I strongly recommend anyone who likes paranormal dragon stories read this. Best prequel ever. Off to look for more by this author.'

∼

Old Ozark Gal from Amazon: Five stars: "...for those who enjoy a sizzling relationship without the graphic descriptions of what body part goes where, this is an excellent book. So what are you waiting for? Go read it!"

∼

Karyn-Anne from Amazon: Five stars: "The romantic scenes were full of passion and heat, but not graphic or explicit. I really, really enjoyed this novella ... Very highly recommended!"

∼

Ahmari from Amazon: Five stars: "This book is very well written ... I liked it so much I purchased the sequel! ... a unique idea for a fantasy and told in a delightful manner. I look forward to reading more from this author."

∼

Praise for *Her Highland Laird*:

Katharina from Amazon: Five stars: "I'm normally not someone who reads romance novels, but … I stumbled over Debbie Mumford's Romance stories. This one was an absolute treat. Not only did it depict the life in 15th century correctly (well researched for such a short story), it evokes emotion very well … I'll definitely read more by this author."

~

Tony from Amazon: Five stars: "Very interesting story. With some suspense and an interesting thread of love."

~

Praise for *Second Sight*:

Bookgirl from Amazon: Five stars: "A lost love, a new love, psychic magic, a murder and a tiger! Wow. I loved this book. It was fast paced and easy to read. I got caught up in the "I'll just read one more chapter" syndrome and lost a bit of sleep but it was worth it. I hope Ms. Mumford writes more in this world. I love these characters."

~

Dragon Slayer from Amazon: Five stars: "I liked the characters and the story line. For those that love a mystery and a good romance along with the paranormal, this book is for you."

For everyone who's ever dreamed that magic was real...

*H*igh Magic called, and Dylan Kincaid obeyed.

Leaving his physical body tucked safely in his bed in an enchanted fortress on the Isle of Skye, Dylan sent his astral self arrowing to the Chamber of Souls. His spirit sang and he cried out with delight. Centuries had passed since last he'd been called upon to perform his true function, his purpose in life. He could hardly wait to meet the new soul he would shepherd into the fullness of his or her power.

He came to rest in the Chamber of Souls, the anteroom which served as a threshold between the astral plane and the firm solidity of earth. The place where souls bound for developing embryos began their journey into physical reality.

Dylan had been here before. Many times. But the gap between his last visit and this was vast. He'd begun to believe that there would be no more, that he had shepherded the last sorcerer into existence ages ago.

But here he stood, in a long, narrow, high-ceilinged white room lit by a diffuse silvery glow. The Portal of Possibility with its white marble pillars stood open at one end of the hall, and the Portal to Earth waited at the other. A soft golden glow pulsed from the earthly threshold.

Gazing expectantly at the space between the white marble pillars, he noted a figure moving toward him, becoming more distinct the closer it came. He watched as the one-who-would-be approached, reminding himself that her form — for the figure was undeniably female — was an illusion. No physical bodies existed in this threshold between the worlds.

When she reached his astral projection, she stopped, her gaze searching his, seeming to memorize every aspect of his soul. Dylan dropped his gaze and inclined his head slightly.

"My lady," he said quietly. "It will be my honor to guard you until your awakening, and to mentor you thereafter until you attain the fullness of your power."

"Dylan Kincaid," she said. Only those two words. His name. And yet his mind staggered beneath the raw power of those lilting syllables. Her voice was melodic and sweet, but that was only the surface. Underneath was beauty too great to be assimilated by a mortal mind.

Fortunately, Dylan was not mortal.

Nor was this creature he was destined to guard and guide. She would be a compelling force when she came into her own in the human realm.

"I will seek you when my destiny is upon me," she said, granting him a radiant smile. "Until we meet again."

He bowed his head and then straightened to watch as she crossed the chamber and entered the softly glowing portal that led to the quickening embryo of the woman she would become.

Dylan sighed with satisfaction. It had been too long since he had guarded and then guided an *Old One* to their destiny. He was delighted to be about his true calling once again. He stared at the place where she had disappeared, savoring the joy of rekindled purpose. He always took his work seriously, but this child he would guard with special care.

"Blessings upon you, Lady," he whispered before returning to his physical body. When he woke on the morrow, he would find his ward's mother-to-be and take up his duties as guardian to an as-yet-to-be-born *Old One*.

CHAPTER 1

Gwen Vaughan pushed her linguistic textbooks away and stood, stretching the cramped muscles in her lower back. Tucking a loose strand of shoulder length dark hair behind her ear, she glanced around the apartment she shared with Emily Stevens.

The two girls had gravitated to each other during their first day's orientation at the University of Colorado's Boulder campus and had been friends ever since. It's possible their friendship was an "opposites attract" kind of thing — gregarious, fun-loving Emily was about as different from studious, dependable Gwen as you could get — but whatever the reason, they'd remained friends through their undergraduate years.

Today was a perfect example of the differences in their psyches. It was her twenty-second birthday (and a mere three days before Christmas!), and where was Gwen? Out partying with friends? Home on the ranch with Aunt Katie and Uncle Jem?

Nope.

In her apartment. Alone. Studying.

Sighing and shaking her head, Gwen ambled to the kitchen to brew a pot of cinnamon tea and scrounge a blueberry muffin, but she stopped after only a few paces.

Something wasn't right.

The air around her felt thick, and the walls of her apartment looked thinner, almost transparent. But that couldn't be! Walls didn't just disappear. Not without some kind of natural disaster... like an earthquake... and even then they didn't disappear. They crumbled and fell.

She caught herself on a chair, closed her eyes, and concentrated on breathing normally. In and out. Easy. Nothing weird about the air. Her heart wasn't racing like one of Uncle Jem's prize horses. Everything was perfectly normal. She was safe in her apartment. All was well.

She opened her eyes... and lost the little bit of calm she'd gained.

She couldn't be... but it *seemed* like she was encased in a bubble of gelatinous air... while everything around her was thinning and becoming transparent.

Gwen could see through her apartment walls, onto the street outside and, even weirder, her vision went deeper... through the cars and pavement to the heart of the earth. She raised her eyes and saw the outline of her apartment building along with the silhouette of the nearby mountains and beyond... into the infinity of space.

If Emily had reported such a thing, Gwen would have wondered what her friend was high on. But Gwen had never gotten into drugs. Em often teased that the most adventurous thing her roomie had ever ingested was the occasional beer.

Gwen shook her head to clear her vision, but the weirdness persisted.

Was she having a nervous breakdown? Had she studied herself into a collapse?

She should lie down. Close her eyes. Take a nap. When she woke up, this would just be a bad dream. Something she imagined.

The plan of action comforted her. Congratulating herself on the sensible strategy, she turned toward her bedroom... and discovered that her plan might not be completely under her control.

Her legs refused to budge. She was rooted in place, unable to move.

A scream clawed at the back of her throat, but her vocal chords refused to release it. Just as panic threatened to overwhelm her, Gwen heard a calm, reassuring voice telling her to be still; to concentrate on her vision; that she was *not* losing her mind.

Without stopping to wonder where the voice came from, Gwen grabbed the hope it offered, and obeyed... and discovered that when she calmed her mind, a golden light appeared, pulsing in the distance. She concentrated on that light — and everything between her and its pulsing glow dissolved. Framed in the center of that golden light she saw a man on horseback.

He sat his bay horse like a man accustomed to the saddle, relaxed, the reins held loosely in one hand. A few years older than Gwen, maybe around thirty, he wore western clothes: denim jeans, blue checkered shirt under a dark leather duster, cowboy boots, and a well-worn Stetson. Chestnut curls escaped beneath the brim of his hat and a red bandana wrapped his neck.

As though feeling her gaze upon him, he turned in the saddle and stared directly into her eyes. A slow smile spread across his tanned face and he mouthed the words, "Well done."

The moment she understood his words, her world snapped back to normal. The return was so sudden, so complete, that she wondered for a moment if she had truly experienced anything out of the ordinary.

Yet, the path between herself and the horseman was indelibly etched in her brain. Though she'd never been there in this life, Gwen knew she would be able to find the place, and the man, without effort.

More importantly, she knew that she would find him, that she *must* find him... and without delay.

*a*s she turned her red Jeep Cherokee north onto US 40, Gwen reviewed the conversation she'd just had with Aunt Katie.

"Guinevere Enid Vaughan, what do you mean you won't be home for Christmas?"

"I didn't say I wouldn't be home at all. I just said I'm going to be delayed a couple of days. I'm sure I'll be there by Christmas Eve." Gwen certainly hoped she was telling the truth.

Aunt Katie and Uncle Jem had raised Gwen since her parents' death. Katie and Jem had been wonderful substitute parents, and Gwen definitely didn't want to worry or disappoint them.

"I got an unusual call from a friend in the mountains, and I need to go check things out. I'll keep in touch and you have my cell phone number." That last had been a stretch. It really had been an unusual call... just not the type Aunt Katie was undoubtedly imagining.

But was it from a friend?

The voice in her mind had left her feeling calm and the smiling face had been reassuring, but this compulsion to obey unknown directives was disquieting. She fervently hoped the man was a friend.

But the real question was: why did she so naively assume that the voice and the face belonged to the same person?

There was only way to find out. She had to follow her vision. Very likely she was on a wild goose chase. The canyon and the man probably didn't exist, but she had to know for sure.

When she reached the turn-off to Raven's Mountain, the road dwindled from asphalt to gravel to dirt before finally disappearing into a simple game trail. Smiling with grim determination Gwen forged ahead, glad to be driving a vehicle capable of handling off-road conditions. Thanks to her vision, she knew the opening to a box canyon waited just ahead, a box canyon she'd never seen. Had never even imagined before this morning's strange events.

When she arrived, she discovered the mouth of the canyon to be very narrow. Barely wider than the shallow stream running through it. At this time of year, the stream itself was little more than ice. Gwen parked the Jeep next to its crystalline surface and made her way into the canyon.

Just as she was about to step into the canyon itself, she encountered another gelatinous membrane, much like the one she'd experienced in her apartment that morning. Pausing for a moment, she wondered if she should risk pushing through, or simply turn around and go home.

Life was good. She had a family who loved her, a field of study that challenged her, and friends who kept her engaged and happy. Why should she risk all of that to follow the directions of a voice and vision about whose origins she had no clue?

She glared at the gelatinous membrane. She didn't have enough information to base a decision on. Particularly not a potentially life altering decision.

And yet...

And yet she knew in her heart that she'd made her decision before she even left her apartment.

She would push past the barrier because she had to know what was on the other side. Had to know if the face and voice were pieces of the same whole. Had to know why this compulsion drove her.

Taking a deep breath, Gwen stepped through the barrier...

...and found herself in a sunny meadow.

On the other side of the membrane it was a briskly cool December afternoon, a skiff of snow dusting the ground and flocking the surrounding pines. In here summer reigned, complete with a profusion of high country wild flowers. Outside the stream was sluggish under a cover of ice; inside it burbled merrily. Gwen frowned, wondering why the water hadn't backed up and flooded the entrance to the canyon?

The canyon itself was enclosed by tall granite cliffs. At the far end, a waterfall sparkled where the stream catapulted over the upper edge of a cliff and cascaded to the canyon floor. The center of the canyon was a meadow filled with flowers in full bloom; around the edges stood tall pines and aspen in full leaf. Near the back, by the waterfall, a small, neat cabin rested against the wall of the canyon. A man sat astride a well-cared for bay horse at the gate to a corral. As she watched, he patted the horse's neck and, urging him forward, cantered to meet her.

He reined to a stop a few feet from her. As she'd expected, he was the man she'd seen in her vision.

"You made good time" he smiled. "I wasn't sure you'd make it today."

Gwen struggled not to burst out laughing. The ordinariness of the statement was so completely out of place. She wasn't sure what she'd been expecting, but it wasn't a mundane conversation. As she struggled with an almost hysterical need to giggle, the horseman dismounted and held out his hand to her. "Dylan Kincaid," he said. "It's nice to finally meet you, Guinevere."

Words gushed from her. "How do you know my name? Where are we? What happened this morning? Why am I here?"

Dylan roared with laughter, then held his hands up as he met Gwen's angry gaze. "Whoa. I'm sorry, but one question at a time, please." He offered his hand again. "Will you walk with me back to the cabin, or would you prefer to ride?"

"I'm not riding double with a man I don't know. Especially one who won't answer my questions."

He grinned and gave a whistle "I didn't expect you would. Here, you take Lady Jane. I'll ride bareback when Warlock gets here." He stepped back from the mare, offering Gwen the reins. She mounted in one fluid movement and was seated squarely in the saddle when a magnificent roan stallion cantered up to Dylan. He hesitated, holding the stallion's mane and gazing at her quizzically. "Do you want me to shorten those stirrups for you?"

Gwen grinned. "I'll manage. It's not that far."

With her comfort established, Dylan leapt lightly onto Warlock's back.

"I know you've got a million questions," he said as the horses plodded slowly across the uneven ground. "I'll answer as many as I can. Some you'll have to answer for yourself in the months to come. Some answers will only generate more questions. But, I'm your guide, and I'll do my best to get you started on the right path."

Gwen eyed him thoughtfully. How odd was it to be having this conversation on horseback? She'd been riding since she first arrived at the Harrison ranch at twelve. Nearly all of her teen-age traumas had been worked through while galloping across a meadow, mucking out a stall, or grooming a horse. It was almost as if Dylan knew what would put her most at ease. She glanced down at Lady Jane's bobbing head, took a deep breath and asked calmly, "What happened to me this morning?"

Dylan's voice was quiet. "You woke up. No," he continued quickly as Gwen's eyes narrowed. "That wasn't a flip answer. I mean, you came of age, and Guinevere Enid Vaughan — the *Old One* — awoke." He glanced at her before continuing. "Your power sparked and ranged out in search of me. You've always known I was here, just as I've always known where you were. You just weren't conscious of that knowledge until you came of age. It's a form of protection."

When they reached the corral, Gwen allowed the familiar motions of dismounting and unsaddling Lady Jane to occupy her hands and mind. The truly disquieting thing about all of this was that she understood what he was saying. As he spoke, pieces fell into place as if she'd been reminded of distantly remembered images. Gwen didn't even need to ask him what an *Old One* was. She knew. *She* was an *Old One*... a conduit of High Magic... a defender of the balance which was a necessity of life itself on this planet.

"Why do I understand what you're talking about?" Gwen mounted the porch steps, and sat down in a woven willow chair that rested in the shade of the wide overhang. "How do I know you're my mentor?"

Dylan took off his battered cowboy hat, tossed it onto a bench in the corner and sat in a matching chair. "You understand because we're connected to High Magic. Your power is awake and it's drawing knowledge from the source of all knowledge. Humans talk about 'racial memory'... but they're really remembering, in a very rudimentary fashion, this ability to draw upon the source."

"Wait a minute," she cried, "what do you mean 'humans talk about'? We're human, aren't we? I mean, my parents were my parents, weren't they?"

Dylan smiled, "No, and yes. No, we're not truly human, and yes, your parents were your parents.

"Let me explain. We are *Old One*s. We're born to human parents, but we're the result of a highly recessive gene that kicks in when High Magic requires a new worker. No one understands how or why this gene is activated, but when it is a perfectly normal human couple gives birth to what appears to be a perfectly normal human baby."

Dylan paused, studying Gwen's face. "The only thing that isn't normal, is that one of us, an *Old One* already in existence, is aware that a new comrade is on the way from the instant of conception. You recognize me as your mentor because I am your guardian. You acknowledged me in that moment between alertness and sleep, just before your soul entered the fertilized egg and quickened it to life. I have been aware of you ever since — guarding you from a distance and waiting for the day when your power would seek me out. The only other difference is that the new child is exceptionally healthy."

He grinned at her. "If you think back, you'll realize that you've never been sick a day in your life. You've probably never thought about it, but it's undoubtedly true." He leaned closer and spoke in a conspiratorial whisper. "And here's the kicker ... you never will be."

Gwen looked up quickly. "I'll *never* be sick? Now that you mention it, I have been unusually healthy, but... well, never is kind of stretching it, isn't it?"

"We're virtually immortal." Dylan nodded as Gwen's eyes widened. "Oh, we can be killed by malice or accident, but we don't age once we've gained maturity and we are immune to all the illnesses that plague the human race."

"Wow." Gwen sat back, amazed by his words, and even more surprised by her own recognition of their truth. "Why haven't I heard stories about our race?"

"You have. The various mythologies of the world are full of our exploits. The term *Old Ones* is synonymous with magic. Humans think that our knowledge has passed from this world. In reality, we have simply withdrawn from their day to day lives; allowed awareness of ourselves to drain out of their consciousness."

Dylan's eyes glazed, and Gwen knew he was gazing inward. "It's just as well that they've forgotten us." His voice was quiet. He spoke thoughtfully, to himself as much as to her. "They would hate and fear us if they knew we still existed."

He shook his head, clearing the cobwebs from his mind. "We don't have a lot to do with them. Our struggle is with the dark forces of the universe, and while humans can be manipulated by either side, we try to assure that they're noncombatants." He paused, glancing at Gwen with twinkling eyes. "When they do become aware of one of us, they explain the experience away with tales of angels, fairies or aliens. Of course, aliens are the favored explanation in this day and age."

Gwen grinned at him. "I've always wanted to meet an alien. I guess my wish has been granted, though you look awfully normal for the job."

"Looks can be deceiving," he quipped. "I think a several-thousand-year-old cowboy counts as pretty darn alien."

Gwen's jaw dropped. "Several *thousand*? Okay. You win. I'm suitably impressed."

He gave her a sympathetic smile. "I know this is a lot to take in. Why don't you take a walk and assimilate, while I throw some dinner together?"

"That sounds great," she said "but, before I forget… why does it seem to be summer in this canyon when it's winter in the real world?"

"Simple," he said. "Magic. Don't forget, we serve High Magic. You'll understand more after you've done your homework tonight. For now, give yourself a break while I rustle up some grub."

CHAPTER 3

*G*wen sat curled comfortably into a worn leather couch in the living room of Dylan's small cabin. In front of her, a fire crackled and popped merrily in the stone fireplace. Between the couch and the fireplace, a multi-hued braided rug covered the bare bones of the cabin's wood floor. She was at peace.

They had eaten a simple dinner of grilled steak and salad, with fresh fruit for dessert. The atmosphere had been calm. Gwen was amazed by how at ease she was in Dylan's presence. There was no tension; no concern about what he would think of her if she sloshed her drink or got salad dressing on her nose. It was like she had known him since birth, as if he was the big brother who had teased and protected her from infancy. He'd said they'd met before her birth. That was a mind-blowing concept. Gwen wondered whether that was a figure of speech, or if he'd intended that she should take him literally.

"Guinevere Enid Vaughan," boomed a commanding voice from behind her, "the Gramarye requires your presence."

She turned to find Dylan standing in the cabin door. He was no longer the easy-going cowboy of the early evening. Instead, he seemed to tower over her, dressed in flowing silver robes, the hood draped carelessly around his neck. He held what could only be described as a wizard's staff in his right hand, highly polished dark wood as big around as her forearm and topped with a faceted crystal. The crystal caught the flickering firelight and sent refracted rainbows sparkling around the room. He was a truly impressive sight.

Gwen shivered, but rose to meet him, gazing squarely into his clear blue eyes. "I'm ready, Dylan." The calmness of her own voice surprised her. "What does the Gramarye require?"

A slight smile lifted the corners of Dylan's lips as he traced a sigil in the air before her.

Gwen felt a quick rush of power, like a small electric crackle. Glancing down she saw that she was now dressed similarly to Dylan, though her robes were black. Running her hand over the fabric, Gwen wondered briefly what it was. Finely woven, soft, with a lovely fluid drape, it wasn't any fabric she recognized.

"This way, Lady Guinevere." Dylan's voice broke into her reverie. He held the cabin door open for her. Obediently, Gwen walked through it. She waited a moment on the porch for Dylan to take the lead, then followed silently. They wound through the woods following a barely marked trail toward the cliff face. At last Dylan paused before a massive rock, studying Gwen's face intently.

"When you pass through this gate, you will be in a place beyond time." Dylan's voice was hushed, as if they waited in the narthex of a great cathedral. "You may stay with the Gramarye as long as you wish. When you return to this path, no time will have elapsed. You need have no concerns about missing appointments or worrying your family with a prolonged absence. Be at peace.

Rest, if your body requires it. Study diligently. Remember who you are." He smiled reassuringly. "The Gramarye will teach you only what you are ready to understand."

Gwen felt the knot in her stomach loosen a little at his last comment. If this Gramarye would only teach her what she was ready to learn, then it must mean this wouldn't be her only opportunity to study. Okay. She was a good student. She knew how to do research. She could handle this.

Oh God! What was she doing here?

With an effort, Gwen forced her attention back to Dylan and saw that he was outlining a door with the crystal atop his staff. The outline shimmered in the moonlight, as Dylan transferred the staff to his left hand and traced a sigil in the air with his right. Immediately there was a soft whoosh of power and the softly glowing outline became shadowed grooves cut deeply into the face of the living rock.

Bowing, Dylan stepped back from the door. "Lady," he said, "I will await your return."

Gwen looked from Dylan's bowed head to the massive door, took a deep breath and stepped forward. She had no idea how to open the door. There were no handles or knobs on it anywhere. Instinctively, she put her hand out in front of her and the heavy rock entry swung open without so much as a touch. With a last nervous glance at Dylan, she stepped into the cliff face...

...and found herself in a library.

Not a library like the one she used on campus, or the public libraries she had frequented as a child. No, this was the kind of library Gwen had always dreamed of owning. The kind she imagined were common in the homes of English nobility. It was a large room, longer than it was wide and there was wood everywhere. The walls, shelves and floors were all of a highly polished dark wood. Mahogany? Cherry, perhaps? She wasn't sure, but she knew that it gleamed richly, almost seeming to pulse with life.

Of course! The flickering firelight from the hearth was what made the room appear to be a living entity.

And the books. What a treasure!

There were books everywhere she looked. The walls were lined from floor to ceiling with shelves, and the shelves were filled to capacity with books of every description. She saw volumes bound in leather, as well as colorful paperbacks; some were obviously hand-sewn, while others were machine made. The lettering on the spines ranged from gold-leaf to simple printer's type to ornate calligraphy. This was truly a reader's paradise.

Nor did the room forget the body as it indulged the mind. There were comfortable overstuffed chairs, as well as a capacious couch, each with its own reading lamp. The final pieces of furniture in the room were actually its centerpiece. A spacious writing table stood in the heart of the room accompanied by a matching chair. A large book lay open on an ornately carved wooden book stand in the center of the table. Gwen knew without question that this was the book she had come to study. This was the Gramarye.

Casting a longing glance at the filled shelves surrounding her, Gwen walked to the desk and sat down. Without realizing what she did, Gwen reached toward the Gramarye with her right hand and began to trace the pattern of the Celtic knot that decorated the front cover of the tome. The design glowed as her finger traced and blissful warmth radiated up her arm. She was safe and warm, secure in the knowledge that nothing could harm her. She was home, where she belonged. All traces of nervousness and anxiety vanished in that instant.

Her fingers trembling with excitement, Gwen opened the ancient book. It was very large, about a foot and a half square and bound in leather-covered wood, making her glad that its carved stand was angled properly — she wouldn't need to adjust the slant of the book for easier reading.

She touched the first page and was amazed to find that it was hand-lettered parchment, probably done with a quill pen, but that was as far as her conscious analysis went. The book was communicating with her.

Her name appeared on the first page along with a single Celtic knot.

Here was the beginning of her true education. All her long years in public school and university had trained her to study, to be diligent, to work hard to learn. Now she understood that there would be no work involved in this learning; this would be pure joy.

Pulse pounding in anticipation, Gwen traced that first sigil below her name.

Instantly, the sigil was impressed in its entirety in her mind. She knew how to draw it in the air, aligning the stray wisps of power that surround all life on earth. She knew the exact position her finger must be in to begin the sigil, the rhythm of her hand movement and how to end it concisely.

She understood the magic it would produce and all the permutations under which it would be both appropriate and inappropriate to perform this spell. For spell it was. There would be no muttered incantations in the power she would wield; simply elegant hand movements such as a conductor might use to control a large orchestra.

She would weave the strands of power, of magic, and she would use them to create and maintain the balance necessary for the human race to progress toward its destiny.

Eagerly Gwen turned the pages of the Gramarye. Each page presented a new pattern which imprinted itself indelibly on her mind as she traced it for the first time on the ancient vellum.

The volumes of information that pressed themselves into her mind as she made that first physical contact with the Celtic knot on the page were amazing. She had seen knotwork like this many times in her study of ancient manuscripts in the library on campus, but those had simply been lines on paper, pretty designs to decorate the page.

Now she understood that these sigils were actually signs of power in the hands of an *Old One* like herself.

Her wonder and curiosity were awake. She could hardly wait to get back to the library, look up some of those manuscripts and discover if there were messages embedded in those illustrations. Her family had never understood her fascination with linguistics. What was the use of studying forgotten languages? Why had she always been intrigued with such things?

Now she understood. Her fascination with language was part of her *Old One* heritage.

Gwen sat turning pages, tracing sigils and absorbing information. There was nothing to indicate the passage of time. The fire didn't even burn down. This was a magical environment, after all.

Finally, her own body's needs began to impinge on her consciousness. Her bladder was full and her stomach was empty. Pulling her mind reluctantly from the current sigil, Gwen glanced around the room once more, wondering where she could find food and a bathroom... not necessarily in that order.

At once the gleam of a brass doorknob caught her attention in the back of the room between two large bookcases. She stood up, stretched and walked across the room to investigate. Sure enough, the door led into a luxurious bath complete with soaking tub and marble counters. Tempted though she was by the thought of a relaxing soak, Gwen opted to refresh herself and go in search of food.

Returning to the main room, she found a small table set by an armchair near the fire laden with her favorite cheese, a small loaf of brown bread, a bowl of grapes and a pitcher of ice water.

"Wow," she mused aloud, just to hear her own voice, "this place really takes care of you." She glanced at the Gramarye as she ate, but decided that some distance was a good thing at the moment. It felt good to relax in the big chair, nibble on her favorite snacks and let her mind wander over the material she had already learned tonight. She now knew that this night was special in the *Old One* calendar. She had been born on the winter solstice - Alban Arthuan - and there was special power in approaching the Gramarye on any of the eight high festivals of the *Old One* year. She would still have learned had she been introduced to the book tomorrow night, but she was grateful that Dylan had called her to study tonight.

The warmth of the fire, the comforting fullness of her stomach and the corresponding fullness of her mind conspired to lull Gwen into a deep sleep. She slept comfortably in the big chair, while her subconscious mind worked to sort and classify all the information she had absorbed that evening. When she woke at last, she was not only physically refreshed, but she realized she was at ease with her new found powers as well.

She visited the bath once again and gazed at her own reflection in the ornate mirror. The same familiar face stared back her: the same soft brown eyes tinged with gold, the same dark brown hair with auburn lights, the same dusting of freckles across the nose, the same softly rounded chin and cheeks. She felt so different on the inside. Surely there should be some tell-tale mark on her face as well?

She sighed, rinsed her hands and face with cool water, and inspected her reflection again. "Welcome to the world, Guinevere Enid Vaughan. You're an *Old One*, you can do magic, and yes, you *are* awake." She smiled at her own absurdity and returned to the Gramarye.

When she finally closed the book, Gwen was very glad that time wasn't an issue. She had studied, eaten, and rested repeatedly before she decided she was ready to face the world again. It was certainly going to be interesting — discovering how all of this changed her world. What did a twenty-two year old university student, who happened to be an *Old One*, do with her magic? What was her purpose? Perhaps Dylan had the answers. It was time to return to the canyon and seek his guidance.

She stepped through the entrance to find Dylan standing just where she had left him. He smiled, took her hand, and lit the path back to the cabin with his staff.

"Did the Gramarye answer all your questions?" he asked.

"It told me more than I could have dreamed of asking... but no, it didn't answer them all. I'm hoping you can fill in some of the details."

"I'll do my best," he replied, "but as I told you earlier, some of the answers you'll have to discover on your own."

He stopped as they reached the cabin and stood in the glow of light falling from the living room window. "First things first." He gestured for Gwen to stop. "You have studied the Gramarye and are now entitled to wear silver robes on the rare occasions when we actually don them. It's time to put your new knowledge to use. Change the color of your robes."

Panic clawed at Gwen's mind. How could he ask her to perform on demand? Then she relaxed as the correct sigil drifted to the surface of her mind. She traced a small pattern on the sleeve of her robe and saw the color change instantly to match the silver of Dylan's robes.

She glanced up, caught his gaze, and smiled with delight. "I did it."

"Indeed you did," he agreed. "Now, let's change back to our jeans and have some coffee while we talk." He led the way into the cabin as he spoke.

Later, after Dylan had quizzed Gwen on which sigil she would choose in varying situations and she had demonstrated her competence at actually producing the signs, she finally got around to asking him the questions which had caused her to leave the Gramarye library.

"So, now that I know what I am and how to use magic," she began, staring into the fire, "what am I supposed to do? Am I supposed to just go back to campus and finish my senior year like nothing's happened? Or is there something High Magic expects of me?"

"Ah," said Dylan, "weighty questions, indeed. And, I'm afraid I don't have easy answers for you. I have no idea what your fate is. I know that my own function is to guard and guide new *Old Ones*, but I had to discover that for myself many long centuries ago. You will discover your task as well."

"But how do I go about discovering my function? What should I do now?"

Dylan studied her worried face for a moment. "My best advice," he said thoughtfully, "is to think about any revelations you may have had while you were studying the Gramarye. It should have given you a clue. While you ponder that question, I think you should return to your normal routine.

"Go home to your family, celebrate Christmas, enjoy your break from school, and then return to campus ready to complete your degree."

"Just go on as if today never happened?" Gwen stared at him in amazement. "What will I say to my family? I'm not the same person anymore."

Smiling a little sadly, Dylan stood and walked to the hearth. "This is why *Old One* children are kept from knowledge too soon. It's a burden, but it's one you're capable of carrying. You're an adult now. Your power is awake and it will guide you. If you find yourself in a situation you feel unable to handle, you can always contact me. Use the sigil we practiced earlier and I will link my mind to yours." He crossed to where she was sitting and placed a hand on her shoulder. "It won't be as bad as you're imagining. You still love your family. Any unease you may feel will pass quickly when you're with them again."

Gwen reached up and grabbed the hand on her shoulder. He was her life-line; she held on while a storm of emotions squalled through her mind. When her thoughts quieted, she released his hand and gave him a timid smile. "You haven't let me down yet. I'll trust you on this one. I guess it's time to face the real world again."

CHAPTER 4

wen turned her Jeep onto the final dirt road leading to the ranch. She found that, despite the butterflies in her stomach, she could hardly wait to see Aunt Katie and Uncle Jem. Approaching the ranch as she had hundreds of times over the past ten years, she found it very hard to grasp that *this* time was different. *She* was different.

She wasn't just Gwen anymore. She was an *Old One*; an immortal creature who could see and weave the strands of magic as easily as everyone else could convey thought by manipulating a stream of air past their vocal chords. But talking had always been a part of Gwen's life, magic was new and— now that she was back in familiar surroundings — unbelievable.

Would Katie and Jem sense the difference in her? Would they still love and trust her?

Would she despise them for their lack of ability to see and understand what she had become?

Gwen shook these uncomfortable thoughts from her mind and tried to concentrate on the aunt and uncle she knew and loved.

Katie was tall and willowy with an athletic grace when she was in motion. She had light brown hair with red highlights which she wore long, usually in a ponytail to keep it under control. Her eyes were blue, but with a grey cast that sometimes made them seem green. Katie had a quick wit and an easy smile - both of which had come in handy as she had battled to stay one jump ahead of the preteen "daughter" she had inherited after Gwen's parents' death.

It was hard for Gwen to remember that there wasn't a blood link between herself and Katie. When she stopped to think about it, Gwen realized she was a lucky girl to have been taken in by such wonderful people. Katie had been her mother's best friend. They had known each other since preschool, had gone to college together and had even been in each other's weddings. But life had pulled them in different directions during their young adulthood and they'd not remained close. Oh, Katie had been aware when Deirdre had given birth to Guinevere, had even seen the young family on a couple of occasions when their paths had crossed, but she had not been a frequent participant in Gwen's early childhood. Even so, Katie had not hesitated to take Gwen in when she had been made aware of Deirdre and Kenneth's tragic deaths.

Not for the first time, Gwen wondered why her parents had died. But this time her thoughts took a new direction. Why *had* her parents died? Dylan had said it was his responsibility to guard her as she grew. Wouldn't that naturally include guarding her parents as well? Keeping her nuclear family safe and intact? Where had Dylan been? Gwen had been in the car when it had been struck head-on by the drunk driver. She had been in mortal danger as well as her parents.

He should have been there.

An uncontrollable rage built in Gwen's mind. The pressure was intense, almost unbearable. Quickly, she guided the Jeep to a stop on the empty dirt road, yanked the door open and sprang out. Glancing wildly about, she searched for something to vent this anger on before the dam of her self-control totally collapsed under the onslaught of waves of righteous indignation. Fastening her attention on a large boulder in the field across the road, Gwen traced a sigil in the air and watched as the boulder disintegrated with a satisfying explosion. Ducking to avoid the flying debris, she sketched a second sigil to vaporize the lethal fragments.

Feeling somewhat foolish, but greatly relieved, Gwen dropped the Jeep's tailgate and sat. She was uncomfortably aware that she had just exhibited a very uncharacteristic level of violence. She had always considered herself to be a calm, rational person.

What was happening to her?

Whatever. She couldn't afford to start having temper tantrums. Not if she had the power to vaporize matter. The stakes were simply too high.

Maybe meditation would help. Did *Old Ones* meditate?

Who knew? Certainly not her, but she'd find out!

Calmer now, Gwen returned to her memories of the night her parents died. She didn't relish the idea of raising her anxiety level again, but knew there were questions that needed to be explored.

She sat with her head in her hands, massaging her scalp, and reviewed her memories.

Think.

You're alive... you didn't die — even though Mom and Dad did.

You can be killed, 'by accident or malice'... I think that's what he said. The accident was a serious enough to kill you. Why are you alive? He must have been there. Remember.

As if conjured by her thoughts the image of a uniformed police officer floated into her mind... and just as quickly floated out again.

"Wait." Gwen commanded. Taking a deep breath, she forced her mind to calmness and looked again at the painful memory of that long-ago night. She remembered sitting on the side of the road where she had flown, as if by magic... her mind balked at the thought, but she forced herself to continue... watching as the family car burst into flames.

That didn't happen in the real world. Cars only burst into flames on impact in Hollywood movies. Nevertheless, her car, and the car of the drunk driver, had both been consumed by flames before her very eyes.

It had been horrible.

Yes, but what else happened?

Gwen narrowed her focus and forced her mind to examine the scene more closely.

There he was. A young man in the blue uniform of a police officer running toward her. Odd... there were no sirens, no flashing lights other than the obscenely dancing flames, yet a police officer was there, bending over her... tracing a sleep sigil before her eyes... staring at her with terror and relief mingled in those clear blue eyes...

Dylan!

He *had* been there. He had removed her from the car at the moment of impact; she was sure of it. Dylan had blurred her memory and put her to sleep, but not before she had seen the fear in his eyes. What had happened? What had caused him to lose control, to allow the death of her parents?

Suddenly, she was very anxious to get home again. Gwen had never questioned Katie and Jem about how they had come to take her in. When she had first arrived, the pain had been too raw, and later it hadn't really mattered.

But now...

Now there were questions burning to be answered.

Gwen hopped down from the tailgate, slammed it shut, dusted off her jeans and got back in the driver's seat. She'd find no more answers in her own memories. Now she needed information that only Katie and Jem could provide. She wanted as much certain knowledge as possible before she confronted Dylan on the matter.

When she came within sight of the ranch at last, Gwen breathed a happy sigh. She was home. The neat white farmhouse with its two story frame and wide porch running the length of the front of the house had never looked so good. The bright, cheerful red front door and the rich Pennsylvania Dutch blue shutters framing all the windows were a welcome sight. Aunt Katie had hung a large evergreen wreath on the front door, and there were candles in all the windows, electric of course, but the effect was warm and welcoming.

The garage behind the house wasn't visible to approaching guests, but Gwen knew it held an older Jeep Wagoneer as well as the ranch pick-up truck. The drive circled in front of the house, with a spur around the right-hand side leading to the garage. She pulled into the circle and parked in front of the wide porch.

As she stepped out of her vehicle she paused, confused. Why wasn't the front door opening in welcome? Where were the dogs? They should be jumping happily around her legs, vying to be the first to lick her hands, or better yet, her face. The silence in the yard was unnerving.

Her newly awakened magical senses screamed at her to be on guard. Even without their warning, Gwen knew that something was terribly wrong. The old Gwen would have rushed into the house calling her family's names.

The *Old One* stood rooted to the spot, extending tendrils of awareness. Concentrating on Katie and Jem, Gwen threw her power in search. Instantly, she entered the gelatinous bubble, and everything fell away between her and her aunt and uncle. They were standing in the barn, about a quarter mile behind the house. The vacant expressions in their eyes told her that this was not just morning chores.

Snapping her mind back to her body, Gwen reviewed defensive sigils while walking quickly to the barn. She wondered whether she should call out to Dylan, but even as the thought occurred, she was aware that he was with her. If she was in trouble, Dylan knew. The knowledge that she was not alone bolstered her confidence, but it also confirmed her suspicion that *something* had happened to interfere with his protection on the night of her parents' death.

No matter. The past was past.

Right now Gwen knew that together they could handle whatever was waiting.

When she came in sight of the barn she saw that a large pavilion had been set up in front of it. The sides were rolled up to let the breeze blow through, and a woman sat on a large, very ornate throne. Coming closer, Gwen saw that the woman was exceedingly beautiful. Her raven black hair fell in waves to her waist, her skin was pale peach perfection and her mouth was full and naturally red. She looked like an expensive porcelain doll. It was the eyes that ruined the image of loveliness. They were blue ice.

Cold and cruel. She didn't need to say a word, her eyes spoke volumes.

"Greetings, Lilith." Gwen's voice was steady, despite the tremor which she felt running the length of her body. "What brings you to my family home?"

Lilith's eyes widened in surprise, then narrowed. "I'm impressed that you know my name, little one." Her voice was clear and melodic, but the overtones were as cold as her eyes. "I've come to welcome you into your power, *Old One*."

Gwen smiled, unwilling to allow fear to distract her. "I'm new to my power, that's undeniable, but I've been well prepared. The Gramarye taught me the names and faces of all my fellow *Old Ones* — even those who have removed themselves from the ranks of the blessed." She paused, drawing strength from her new-found knowledge. "You are not welcome here, Lilith. Depart."

Cheeks flaming with anger, Lilith sprang from her throne. "Brave words, child. Tread lightly. I am powerful, and experienced beyond your ability to comprehend. But," her tone lightened, " I am not here to threaten you. I am here to make you an offer." She smiled, a cold grimace that never touched her eyes.

"If you are here in friendship," Gwen replied calmly, "then why are my aunt and uncle locked in stasis in the barn?"

"Merely a precaution." Lilith gave dismissive wave of her elegant hand. "I simply wanted to ensure a private conversation with my new comrade."

"I doubt we're going to be comrades," said Gwen. "Release them and we'll go elsewhere to have our private chat."

"I think not." Lilith stepped from the pavilion and strolled toward Gwen. "I don't like your attitude. I was going to release them, but now I think hostages are a fine way to keep you in line. You must learn to approach your elders with more respect. Especially one like myself — who comes to help you develop your power."

Gwen choked back a quick retort, sighed and spoke in the most diplomatic tone she could muster. "What are you proposing, Lilith?"

"That's more like it," Lilith purred, her ego stroked by Gwen's obvious struggle to control her words. "I'm here to offer you the chance to become a goddess. Join your power to mine. Forget High Magic. It only uses us as tools, pawns to advance the fates of these mortals. Why should we, who are powerful magical creatures, be chained to nursemaiding these insipid humans? They should worship us. They should exist only to do our bidding. Why, their life spans are ridiculously short. Think what we could accomplish without High Magic's interference. Join me, and be adored." Her cold eyes sparkled with excitement at the thought of the supposed adoration in which she would be held.

"I'm sorry to disappoint you, Lilith, but I don't want to be worshiped. I care deeply for many of these mortals. Besides, before yesterday, I thought I *was* mortal. I'm not ready to scorn them… and I hope I never will be." As she spoke, Gwen searched her mind for Dylan's presence. The calm reassurance that flooded her consciousness told her that he would soon be there physically as well as psychically. Unsure whether or not she should attempt to take offensive action, Gwen watched Lilith carefully. She was grateful that both of Lilith's hands remained visible as she resumed her seat on the throne.

Stay calm, Gwen. Dylan's voice whispered through her mind. *Reinforcements are about to arrive. Don't make any sudden movements.*

The gentle breeze which had been playing around the pavilion suddenly strengthened. Gwen felt a brief electric tingle, then became aware of beings materializing in a large circle surrounding herself and the pavilion.

Lilith, unconcerned with Gwen's fledgling power, was caught off guard by the sudden appearance of her peers.

"Well, Dylan," she sneered, " you seem to be taking your duties more seriously this time. Greetings, fellow *Old Ones*. I wish I could say this was a pleasure."

The circle pulsed with magical energy, and Gwen was startled to realize that her rescuers had encased them all in one of those gelatinous bubbles. She was now enclosed in a warded sphere. No stray magic would escape to concern the human world.

"You are contained, Lilith." Dylan's voice rang with satisfaction. "You cannot fight us all, and you cannot harm the mortal realm from inside this sphere."

"True enough, Dylan," Lilith answered calmly, "but I would call it a stand-off. While I am contained in the sphere, my magic cannot sustain the mortals I hold captive in the barn. They are suffocating as we speak. Tell me, Guinevere," she caught Gwen's gaze and held it, "are you willing to sacrifice your family merely to contain my power for a time?"

"Dylan?" Gwen cried out in panic, never taking her eyes from Lilith's cruel face.

As one, the *Old Ones* surrounding her allowed the magical sphere to dissipate. Gwen raced into the barn to find her aunt and uncle alive, but unconscious, on the packed dirt floor. Glancing back through the open doors, she saw Lilith trace a sigil in the air and disappear with a triumphant laugh. The pavilion remained, mute testimony to the validity of the entire experience.

Having checked Aunt Katie's vital signs, Gwen turned her attention to Uncle Jem. He was long and lean, and the absence of the wiry strength that was his usual trademark was unnerving. Gwen tenderly brushed the greying black hair from his forehead before picking up his rough, calloused left hand. She felt tears prickle under her eyelids as she willed his warm brown eyes to open and see that she was with him.

Gwen was so focused on Jem that she was unaware of the other *Old Ones* milling about the barn until she felt a hand on her shoulder. Glancing up, she watched as a handsome young man knelt at her side.

"They will recover." He laid a hand lightly on her shoulder, and Gwen felt a wave of sympathy brush her mind. "I'm sorry you've had such a rough introduction to our world. Try to remember, you never have to be alone. We, your brothers and sisters, are only a thought away." With that, he stood... and vanished before her eyes.

Suddenly the barn felt empty. The magical power that had filled it dissipated and Gwen realized that of all the *Old Ones*, only Dylan remained.

CHAPTER 5

"I just can't imagine what happened," Aunt Katie repeated for the third time. "Why would Jem and I both pass out at the same time?"

"Don't worry about it, Aunt Katie." Gwen patted her hand and willed the anxiety to pass. "I'm sure it was just a fluke. I'll ask my friend Dylan to test the barn for noxious fumes. He studies that kind of thing at CU."

"I'm so embarrassed that your friend had to be involved in this." Aunt Katie was nearly in tears. "What must he think of us?"

"Stop that. Dylan was very happy to be here, to be able to help out when we needed it. Now, don't give it another thought. I'm going to fix you a hot bath, with candles and soft music. You've had a hard day and you need to relax."

Gwen stood and strode to the master bath. As she filled the tub, arranged candles and found a CD with soothing music, she thought about what Dylan had told her.

"They won't remember Lilith or anything that happened earlier today. I've arranged their memories so they will believe they were just unconscious in the barn. I'll stay until I'm certain there will be no adverse effects. Just introduce me as a friend from Boulder. Once I'm convinced that they're sound, I'll leave and let you and your family have some privacy."

At her alarmed expression, he'd patted her shoulder. "I don't believe Lilith will return, but if she does, I'll know. Don't worry, they'll be protected."

He had stayed for an hour or so, helping Gwen get Katie and Jem back to the house, covertly testing their memories and reflexes as he introduced himself and helped to make them comfortable. Then he had stepped outside with Gwen and, after helping her ward the house, had simply vanished. There had been no opportunity for her to question him about her parents, and in truth, she hadn't wanted to bring the subject up with him just yet.

After settling Katie in the hot bath, Gwen stepped into the living room to check on Jem. He was stretched out on the couch with a quilt tucked under his chin, sound asleep.

With an approving nod, she allowed herself to sit down in the recliner across from him and relaxed her mind for the first time since her encounter with Lilith. As she closed her eyes, a face drifted into her thoughts. A chiseled face with strong chin, high cheekbones and a long straight nose. It was an attractive face, not handsome enough to draw unwarranted attention, but strong and undeniably masculine.

It was his eyes that commanded Gwen's attention. Deep, rich, chocolate pools whose warmth invited her to lose herself in their depths. The memory of those eyes caused a shiver of delight to run up her spine. Who was this dark haired *Old One* who had spoken to her as she knelt over Uncle Jem? Searching her memory she found the name that matched the face: Lorenzo Santini.

Feeling slightly amused and more than a little embarrassed at her reaction to his remembered face, Gwen decided she'd definitely enjoy getting to know Mr. Lorenzo Santini.

When all three of them were rested and relaxed and enjoying a casual meal of ham sandwiches, chips, and big tumblers of buttermilk, Gwen broached the subject of her parents' deaths.

"Aunt Katie, Uncle Jem, I was wondering as I drove home yesterday... how did I come to live with you?" she asked quietly. "I mean, I know it was because Mom and Dad died, but what was involved?"

Katie and Jem glanced at each other across the table. "We've wondered for years if you would ever get around to asking us about that night." Jem turned his head to observe Gwen as he spoke. "We understood why it didn't come up at first, you were in shock. But we figured, after you got older, you'd eventually want to know all the details."

"I actually kept a sort of diary," Katie mused. "I was afraid I'd forget the little things. As it turns out, they're pretty well seared into my brain." She took a sip of buttermilk and stared at the table. Gwen could almost see her arranging her thoughts. "We got the call about midnight. A young man identified himself as a Portland police officer. He told us Kenneth and Deirdre had been killed in an accident. Said you'd survived. It was a real blow." Katie swallowed hard, then stilled her trembling fingers by gripping her tumbler. "He said they'd found a will naming us as your guardians; asked if we would accept responsibility for you. We did, of course." She smiled across the table at Gwen. "You arrived the next afternoon. We met you at the airport in Denver. A nice young man was with you, said he worked for Portland Social Services."

"I'll say one thing for them," Uncle Jem broke in, "they're efficient out there in Portland. I believe you were safely here with us before your folks had been gone twenty-four hours. I can't imagine that the bureaucracy in Denver would function that quickly."

Gwen kept her eyes on her plate, her voice carefully neutral. The last thing she wanted was to alarm them. "Did you ever see any official paperwork? The will? Did the Portland authorities ever contact you again?"

Jem narrowed his eyes as he considered her questions. "Well, now that you mention it, no... we never did see the will. Weren't ever contacted by any lawyers either. At least, not until the Trust contacted us about a year after we took you. They wanted to let us know there was money for your upkeep, and college, if we needed it."

"The social worker who brought you must have been satisfied with our arrangements," Katie continued. "No one ever came back to check up on you. At the time, I didn't worry about it. But later on, I wondered. I mean, what if we hadn't been fit parents? I guess we must have fallen through the cracks, being out of state and all."

"Turned out okay, though," Jem interjected. "I'm just as happy we didn't have officials snooping around all the time."

Gwen smiled at her aunt and uncle. "It turned out more than okay. I couldn't have wished for a better home." She yawned and stretched. "Well, I think I'll turn in, and you two should get some rest too. We don't want any relapses of whatever happened earlier."

Kissing each of them on the cheek, Gwen left the room and climbed the stairs to her bedroom. Once there, she traced an elaborate sigil around herself and settled into a lotus position on the floor to wait. She'd barely had time to calm her breathing and relax into her position before she felt Dylan's quiet voice in her mind.

You called my lady? he whispered.

I did, Dylan. Thank you for your quick reply.

Mindspeech was a funny thing. If Aunt Katie peeked in, she would see Gwen sitting at peace in her favorite yoga position. Katie would have no idea that Gwen was engaged in serious conversation with her mentor.

I need to talk to you... in person. I want to be able to see your face while we discuss this matter. Gwen felt Dylan's surprise as he agreed to come to the ranch the day after tomorrow.

Tomorrow wouldn't do. Tomorrow was Christmas. Katie and Jem would expect it to be a family day, especially since their family had just experienced a crisis. They had no idea how serious the crisis had been, but they felt the tension, in themselves as well as in Gwen. Instinctively they pulled their family in tight.

Gwen would just have to wait an extra day for the answers she was so anxious to hear. Thanking Dylan for agreeing to come, Gwen terminated the connection with a wave of her hand. It was late, and she was tired. Tomorrow promised to be the most unusual Christmas Gwen had ever known.

CHAPTER 6

*C*hristmas morning dawned crisp and cold. Peeking out her window, Gwen had the errant thought that it looked as if pixies had come in the night and scattered the lawn with diamonds. The snow sparkled brilliantly as it lay awash in the fresh morning light.

Deliberately setting aside all thoughts of *Old Ones* and High Magic, Gwen put on her warm fleece robe and sheepskin slippers and headed downstairs to enjoy the wonder of Christmas morning with her loved ones.

"Oh, Aunt Katie… Uncle Jem. I love it." Gwen was ecstatic over her final present. "Where did you find it?" The torn wrappings had revealed a delicate, antique silver bracelet shimmering regally in a velvet lined case.

Examining the bracelet closely, Gwen saw that the individual links were finely wrought Celtic knots. Sigils to her trained eye, but not just any sigils. These were all forms of protective sigils. Whoever wore this bracelet would be well guarded, for these were not just lovely works of art produced by a talented craftsman. These were active magical symbols. Spells sustained in silver by a powerful *Old One*. She saw the lines of power being pulled into shape by the bracelet, and knew that when she placed it on her wrist, the power would wrap around her like a cocoon.

"I'm so glad you like it, dear." Aunt Katie beamed with delight. "We found it when we went up to ScotsFest in Estes Park last September. It was in an obscure little booth. The vendor saw me looking at her jewelry and pulled this case out from under the table. She said it was very special, and insisted I'd know what to do with it. Well, the minute I saw it, it just seemed to call your name. I knew it had to be your Christmas gift."

Not wanting to be left out, Uncle Jem added his recollections to the tale. "I thought she'd lost her marbles," he said, nodding to his wife. "I'm no expert on jewelry, but even I can tell that's quality... and old. I was afraid to even guess at a price. But Katie was determined and the woman seemed just as anxious for it to come to us. It took some haggling, but she let us have it for a price even I couldn't argue with. Truth be told, I think we got a real deal."

"I'm sure you did, Uncle Jem. I'll cherish this as an heirloom. My first piece of fine jewelry. I'll never take it off. Thank you so much." Gwen slipped the bracelet onto her wrist, watching in fascination as the lines of magic wrapped themselves around her body. She wondered which of her *Old One* brethren had sold this amazing artifact to Katie and Jem. Whoever it was, she must have guessed Gwen would soon need protection.

"This seems to be our year for silver jewelry," Gwen said as she handed a small box to each of them. "These aren't antiques or anything, but I thought you might enjoy wearing them."

Gwen had imbued the silver rings with protective sigils. They didn't hold even a tenth the power of the bracelet on her wrist, but she knew they would be sufficient to warn her if Katie and

Jem were ever subjected to another magical attack. The rings themselves wouldn't be enough to save Katie and Jem if Lilith attacked, but they would draw Gwen and Dylan to the rescue. Gwen was certain that together she and Dylan would be more than a match for Lilith's cunning.

The rings were also spelled to be cherished. Katie and Jem were unlikely ever to take them off. They would find that the rings were unaccountably precious to them, their favorite articles of "clothing."

Dylan arrived the next day about mid-morning. He came to the door, bearing a bouquet of yellow roses which he presented to Katie with a flourish.

"We didn't really get a chance to meet the other day, Mrs. Harrison," he said with a smile, "here's hoping that today will be an uneventful visit." He turned fluidly to Jem and extended his hand, "Mr. Harrison, a pleasure, sir."

Jem took his proffered hand in a firm grip, then turned to gaze at Gwen. "I don't know where you found this young man, honey, but you're welcome to bring him around any time."

Gwen blushed and found herself momentarily tongue-tied. Dylan gallantly came to the rescue. "Guinevere is a lovely young woman, Mr. Harrison, but we are merely colleagues at the university. This isn't a romantic relationship."

Uncle Jem looked skeptical, but made no further comments.

"Please, come in and make yourself comfortable, Mr. Kincaid," Aunt Katie smiled at Dylan before turning a stern gaze on Uncle Jem. "What can we do for you today?"

"Please, call me Dylan," he replied with a charming grin, "and I apologize for interrupting your holiday, but I need to talk to Guinevere about her senior thesis. There are some preliminary notes she needs to look into before the next term begins. Is there somewhere that we could discuss our boring linguistics without any further inconvenience to you folks?" Dylan's smile was both warm and ingratiating. Katie quickly ushered them into a small den off the family room, which served as the ranch office.

"Just let me know if you'd like coffee or anything." Katie was clearly impressed with her niece's guest. "Gwen knows where all the office supplies are, if you need pens or paper or anything like that."

"Thank you, Mrs. Harrison, we'll be just fine in here." Dylan had won her over so completely, that Katie didn't seem to notice she had been dismissed in her own home. She closed the door quietly and left them to their business.

Dylan turned to Gwen, indicated chairs and sat down. "What can I do to help you, Lady Guinevere?"

Gwen curled into a dark leather wingback chair and regarded Dylan thoughtfully. Now that he was sitting in front of her, she found herself less angry, less ready to judge his actions. He was the first and firmest link Gwen had to her new life, to her destiny. He had done nothing but help her in the last few days, and she had been greatly in need of help. Consciously, Gwen willed her mind to a calm state, then cleared her throat and began.

"Dylan, ever since I left the Gramarye I've been remembering things... about the night my parents died." She closed her eyes for a moment, took a deep breath, and continued, "These new memories, and my own logic, have led me to believe you can tell me exactly what happened that night." Gwen looked up to find Dylan sitting perfectly still, his eyes closed and his face slack. Frightened for him, she cried out, "Dylan?"

His eyes flew open and he gave her a chagrined smile. "I'm fine, Guinevere. I heard every word you said, but I must confess, I was mindspeaking another *Old One* as you spoke." The confused, hurt expression on her face caused him to hurry with his explanation. "There was someone else deeply involved in the events of that night. If you have no objection, I'd like to invite him to join us."

Feeling totally bewildered, Gwen nodded her head. This was what she wanted after all. She wanted to know the truth. All of the truth.

Dylan acknowledged her assent with a small smile and closed his eyes again. A moment later, Gwen was aware of another presence in the room and turned quickly to see a man standing in the corner behind her chair.

"Lady Guinevere." The man nodded to Gwen as he stepped out of the shadows. "Dylan. The moment of reckoning has come more quickly than I anticipated." He gave her a wry smile. "I thought it would be several months before your mind stopped reeling from new information and allowed you to inspect old wounds."

"Mr. Santini." Gwen acknowledged his presence from the safety of Uncle Jem's favorite chair. "I thank you for your time, though I don't understand your role."

Dylan conjured a third chair for Lorenzo and performed an intricate sigil around him. Gwen watched curiously. "For your aunt's benefit." Dylan answered her unspoken question. "If she returns, she won't see him, but will avoid this part of the room. It will save awkward explanations and the need to amend her memory."

Lorenzo recalled their attention to the matter at hand. "I believe you were just beginning to question Dylan about the night you were orphaned. Let me go back a bit further and tell you that, until your birth, I was the youngest *Old One*. Dylan was also my mentor, and as such he retained a certain parental protectiveness toward me."

"True," Dylan broke in, "though my responsibilities to Lorenzo ended several hundred years ago, he was my most recent protege, and I remain concerned about his safety."

"Several hundred years." The words burst from Gwen's mouth before she could think about their propriety. "Has it been that long since one of us was born? When you said we were rare, I thought you meant every fifty years or so."

Both Dylan and Lorenzo looked startled. Lorenzo recovered first. "I was born in the year of our Lord 1430," he said, "just in time to come into my power and be ready to take on my first pupil, Leonardo da Vinci. But we stray from the topic."

Dylan nodded and took up the narration. "Indeed. The night your parents died, Lorenzo was under attack. Magical attack. The *Old Ones* from this part of the world gathered to defend him, and though you were my primary responsibility, my desire to protect my former student got the better of me. I left you in the safety of your warded home and went to Lorenzo's defense."

It's well that he did," Lorenzo continued soberly, "even with Dylan's considerable power added to the mix, we were barely able to come out with our lives. Unfortunately, we didn't realize that the attack on me was a diversion. A very costly diversion in terms of magic expended, but a diversion nonetheless. You were the true target."

Gwen jumped in her chair. "Me? Who would be interested in me? I was twelve years old at the time. I had no idea I was an *Old One*. Who would want to kill me?"

Dylan sighed. "Lilith," he stated simply. "She and her group of Dark Ones had been studying prophecy and had determined that you were a threat to their desire for power. Even as a child, your magical aura was very strong. Any magical being couldn't help but be aware of your existence. That was a sticky problem for Lorenzo and me after the attack. But we're getting ahead of ourselves."

At that moment there was a light tap on the door and they all froze. Aunt Katie stepped into the room carrying a tray of food. "I thought you might like some snacks." Gwen watched her aunt navigate carefully around Lorenzo with no apparent awareness of the circuitous path she took through the room. "Do you two need anything else?" She smiled at Dylan, placing the tray on the large walnut desk.

"Oh, this looks just wonderful. Thank you so much." Gwen gave Katie a bright smile. "This is a sticky point we're discussing. It may be another hour or so before we finalize our plans."

"Okay. I'll leave you to your strategy session." She kissed Gwen on the top of her head and left the room.

Lorenzo sighed. "You certainly haven't lost your touch with the *I'm not here, don't pay attention to me* sigil, Dylan."

Gwen nodded her agreement. "It was fascinating to see that in action." She shook her head to clear it from Katie's interruption. "Okay, let me see if I'm following you so far. Lorenzo was under deadly attack, so Dylan left me at home with wards in place and went to the rescue." Both men nodded. "Then Lilith attacked me as well? How?"

Dylan and Lorenzo exchanged glances, and spoke simultaneously.

"We're really not sure," said Dylan.

"We don't know," muttered Lorenzo.

Gwen glanced at each in turn. "All right. Tell me what you *do* know."

"We know that for some unknown reason your parents decided to go somewhere in the car. We have no idea where they were going, or why, but I'm guessing the idea was planted with a compulsion spell. When I left they were settling in for the night."

"I don't understand, Dylan," Gwen said with a puzzled frown, "you talk like you were there in the house with us."

"You don't remember me, but I lived next door. I rented the apartment over your neighbors' garage. I was close enough to guard you, to *nudge* your parents in the right direction when I felt it necessary. I worked as a free-lance writer in those days, so no one thought it strange that I was around the neighborhood all day. I often went for long walks, and sat for hours writing in a notebook in the park across the street from your school. I was never very far from you physically, except the night Lorenzo was attacked."

As he spoke, Gwen remembered the reclusive neighbor he described, an oddity to be sure, but just part of the landscape of her childhood. She wondered if he had used the *I'm not here, don't pay attention to me* sigil on the whole neighborhood.

"Anyway," Dylan continued, "we just about had the attack on Lorenzo under control when I felt an incredible spike of fear from you, a psychic scream... "

"Yes," agreed Lorenzo, "it was so strong all of us heard it and knew who it was, even though Dylan was the only one who had ever touched your mind. You've got one heck of a psychic punch."

Dylan ignored him as he continued his narrative. "I immediately teleported to you. I arrived just in time to remove you from the car before the crash. Unfortunately, I was too late to save your parents. The other driver was beyond my help as well. I altered my clothes to a police uniform, in case there were any witnesses, and ran to where I had placed you — under a tree in a neighboring yard.

"You were unharmed, but in shock from what had just happened. I altered your memory, so you wouldn't remember hovering in the air and being gently deposited on the ground, but didn't touch your thoughts about the accident itself. Then I simply removed you from the scene. When the real police arrived, they had no reason to think there had been more than two people in your car."

"So, it was you who contacted Katie and Jem. You brought me to Colorado." Gwen nodded to herself as the puzzle pieces began to arrange themselves into a complete picture. "Didn't the authorities in Portland wonder what happened to me?"

Dylan almost blushed. "They didn't know you existed," he said quietly.

"When he realized the severity of the accident, Dylan called in reinforcements." Lorenzo continued the story, giving Dylan a moment to collect his thoughts. "Many volunteered to help, but I'm the one he chose. I took you to a safe place and cared for your wounds. Emotional wounds," he added quickly as distress clouded her features, "while Dylan made the necessary adjustments to your home and neighborhood."

Dylan picked up the thread. "I removed all evidence of you from your home, and from your neighbors' minds. I only needed them to forget you for a day or two, so I used a temporary sigil. They forgot about you just long enough to satisfy the authorities that there were no loose ends needing to be tidied up. When you floated back into their memories, they assumed you had died with your parents... such a tragedy."

"When it was all arranged," said Lorenzo, "I got us seats on a flight to Denver and brought you to Katie and Jem, posing as a social worker. Once you were in their care, we could finally breathe a sigh of relief."

"But, why?" That was all Gwen could think to ask. "Why go to all that trouble? Why not just let the police and social services do their jobs?"

Dylan watched her carefully, his eyes full of compassion. "Because, we needed to hide you from Lilith. You were still in danger. We knew we wouldn't be able to hide the fact that you had survived, but we were determined to hide *you*."

"That was another thing I did," Lorenzo commented. "While I was working to lessen the impact of your trauma, I put a filter on your natural psychic gift. I effectively hid you from magical detection. It dissipated when your power awoke, but until then, it kept Lilith from locating you."

"Once I had talked to Katie and knew she would accept you," Dylan continued, "I removed all traces of Katie's connection to Deirdre. The authorities didn't know you existed, the neighbors thought you were dead, and there were no clues in the house to lead to Katie and Jem. We made you disappear."

"Then we held our breath, to see if we'd overlooked any insignificant detail that would endanger you." Lorenzo finished with a quiet exhalation of breath.

Gwen sat quietly, thoughts running wild in her mind. As she began to corral them, to achieve some mental order, she realized that both Dylan and Lorenzo were studiously watching her face.

She unfolded out of her comfortable leather chair and knelt in front of Dylan. Taking his hands in hers, she gazed deeply into his eyes. "Thank you for my life, Lord Dylan. Forgive me for doubting your devotion to duty... and to me." She leaned forward and kissed his cheek.

From where she knelt, she reached for Lorenzo's hand. "Thank you also, Lorenzo. Not only for the past, but for coming to my family's defense this week." She took a deep breath and continued, still holding each man's hand. "I pledge to you both that I will be worthy of the effort and concern you have expended on my behalf."

As she spoke the words a delicate melody floated through their minds and Gwen knew that High Magic had accepted her pledge as a binding covenant.

She wondered what High Magic would require of her as proof of her resolve.

CHAPTER 7

$\mathcal{I}$t was a beautiful winter day in Boulder, Colorado. The foothills wore their armor of tall pines proudly, and the flatirons stood like shields, protecting the mountain god's breast. The light dusting of snow on the evergreens emphasized their dark beauty, while the blue of the sky was so brilliant it almost hurt the eyes.

Gwen gloried in her surroundings, reverently acknowledging the power pulsing around and through her. Now that she was fully awake, it amazed her that she could have walked these paths and been unaware of the magical energy radiating from the mountains. On a clear, cold day like this, the power was almost palpable. It was certainly no surprise to her now that so many people chose to make this area their home. Boulder sat in the shelter of a potent magical node formed by the intersection of several lines of power.

Breathtakingly beautiful though the day was, it was also bitingly cold, and Gwen was glad to reach the warmth of the linguistics building. Consciously she clamped her mind around the nervousness that was making her stomach twist in knots. There was nothing to fear here. This was her home on campus. She had spent so much of her nearly four years in this building that she knew every nook and cranny. She gazed fondly at the polished wood and stone of the hallway and main staircase, and was surprised to find a familiar figure striding toward her.

"Good morning, Miss Vaughan," he said as he approached, "if you would follow me, please."

Gwen swallowed her astonishment, arranged her face in a studious mask and fell into step beside Dylan as he marched down the corridor toward the wing that housed the professors' offices.

When they finally stopped, it was in front of a door she had walked past many times on her way to counseling sessions with her advisor. Now she studied the gold letters on the frosted glass and started. *Dylan Kincaid, Ph.D.*, the door proclaimed to any and all who bothered to look.

Dylan opened the door and walked in, motioning for Gwen to have a seat.

"Have you always been here?" Gwen asked, her voice slightly belligerent as she eyed Dylan suspiciously. "Or did you charm your way onto campus recently?"

He studied her as he sat behind at his desk. "I've been here ever since you first set foot on campus. As soon as you sent in your letter of intent to enroll as a freshman, I applied to the Dean of this department for a position. He was so excited by my credentials that he hired me on the spot." He grinned at her expression of wary disbelief. "Longevity and magic are an unbeatable combination when it comes to supporting yourself."

"Why haven't I seen you before?" There was a definite growl to her voice as she removed her backpack and dropped it on the floor next to her chair.

"Oh, you probably have." Dylan waved a dismissive hand in the air. "I teach in the graduate division, so our paths haven't crossed in the classroom. That was always my intention. I wanted to be close enough to protect you without being so close that I smothered your instincts."

"Fine. So why are we meeting now?" Gwen's irritation at finding Dylan here, in her home away from home, was irrational, but that didn't make it any less real.

"Really, Miss Vaughan." Dylan raised an eyebrow and cocked his head. "Don't you pay attention to your mail when you're on break? You should have received a note from Dr. Emerson letting you know he had recommended you for independent study with one of the graduate professors. I am that professor, and we are here to discuss the form your senior thesis will take."

Gwen had the good grace to blush, and she stumbled over her next few words. "Sorry, sir. Of course I got the letter. I was on my way to this room when we met. I just hadn't realized that the Dr. Kincaid in room #146 would be you."

Dylan laughed and threw a pencil at her. "Relax, Guinevere. This is all part of the plan. You will legitimately complete your degree by the end of this semester. However, with me in control of your schedule, your, um... conflicts of interest should be minimized."

Gwen caught the pencil and stared at him in bewildered silence.

"This won't be an easy semester for you. Not only will you complete your senior thesis under my tutelage, but you will also be studying magic. It is my intention that you discover your unique ability as well as your purpose before you leave this institution. You will essentially be doing twice the amount of work of your fellow seniors. But then, the rest of your classmates are no longer in your league."

Gwen squared her shoulders and looked Dylan directly in the eye. "Wonderful, when do we start?" Her expression clouded as a troubling thought occurred to her. "What will I call you? I mean, Dr. Kincaid is just so… formal."

"Call me Dylan," he said soothingly. "I have a reputation with my peers for being very casual with my students. Many of them disapprove, but they can't do anything about my preference for being called by my given name. All my graduate students call me Dylan. There will be nothing remarkable about you calling me that as well."

Gwen felt her two worlds slide into sync and gave Dylan a dazzling smile. From the moment she'd seen him in the corridor, she'd been frightened that he would endanger her equilibrium. Gwen already felt like she was balancing on a high wire, afraid she would slip and say something inappropriate. His presence had aggravated the situation as far as she could see. Now she understood that Dylan had arranged things so that she would be able to blend the two sides of her being in safety, before she left the shelter of her campus cocoon.

The next few weeks were some of the most exhausting and exhilarating of Gwen's life. Dylan set a rapid pace. They met daily to discuss Gwen's progress on her thesis research, as well as her understanding of the volumes of arcane lore he assigned as part of her magical education.

The arcane volumes never left Dylan's office and were carefully warded when neither of the *Old Ones* were present. Consequently, Gwen spent several hours a week sitting alone in his office studying. Dylan had graduate seminars to teach, so she confined her arcane study to the hours he was in class. The rest of her time was fairly evenly divided between research in the large university library and sitting in her apartment in front of her computer trying to arrange her findings into some semblance of order.

"Guinevere Enid Vaughan. You aren't going to spend the entire weekend buried in those books again, are you?" Gwen's roommate, Emily, scolded as she walked into what passed for a study area in their apartment. "Your social life is terminally ill."

"What social life?" Gwen responded without looking up.

"My point exactly." Emily crowed. "You have got to get out of this apartment."

"Right," said Gwen, "I'll be heading out in about an hour."

"Heading where?" Emily asked suspiciously.

Gwen frowned, perplexed. "To the library of course. Where else would I be going?"

Emily stared at her in exasperation. "The library doesn't count as *getting out*. Come on, girl, get your coat. You're coming with me. Don't make me call in reinforcements." Emily pierced her with a scowl as Gwen started to protest. "Kendra and I both have boyfriends who'd be happy to pick you up and carry you out for pizza. Which, by the way, is another topic entirely. When was the last time you went on a date?"

"Emily, for heaven's sake. You know I don't have time for dating. I'm barely getting everything done spending every spare minute in the library. I'd never keep up if I took time out for *dates*."

"That's the problem," Emily pounced, "you're swamped and you won't admit it. You really should go to Dr. Emerson and tell him that this new guy is running you into the ground. Just because he's a big-wig graduate professor and he only takes on an undergrad independent study about once in a blue moon is no reason to let the man kill you."

Gwen smiled at her roommate's description of Dylan and decided that pizza with friends wasn't such a bad idea. She did need to eat, and one evening of relaxation wouldn't throw her schedule completely off kilter. Besides, she could always stretch time if she had to... and tell Dylan it was an exercise in sigil mastery.

THIS WAS A VERY GOOD IDEA, Gwen admitted to herself as she sat in the pizza parlor with her friends. It felt so good to relax and let the flow of their laughing chatter wash over her. Emily, Chad, Kendra and Danny were telling stories about their Christmas breaks, each vying to be more outlandish than the last. They were hilarious and, Gwen was sure, only loosely based on reality. Besides, it was so nice to laugh unguardedly that she didn't care what they'd really done on break.

Gwen contributed to the general giddiness of her table by asking questions and egging the others on, but she was careful not to launch into tales of her own extraordinary adventures over the holidays. She participated enough that the others didn't seem to notice she wasn't actually telling them anything.

Smiling to herself, as her fears melted away, she acknowledged that she could stop avoiding spending time with her friends. She hadn't even needed to resort to nudging their thoughts away from her with magic, though she was comforted to know that the ability to do so was easily within her power.

Gwen wiped tears of laughter from her eyes until she noticed that the noise of the pizza parlor had been silenced by a distinctly unpleasant buzzing in her mind. Instantly on guard, she felt the sigils of her bracelet initiate their protective barrier, cocooning her in pulsing energy. All around her, the occupants of the restaurant sat frozen. The cheese dripping from Emily's pizza slice was even arrested in its plummet toward the plate.

"We meet again, child," Lilith's voice dropped into the silence as she materialized in the aisle next to Chad. Momentarily distracted, she loomed over Chad, stroking his cheek with her index finger. "So young, so handsome... ah well, perhaps later."

Gwen felt panic threaten to overwhelm her. She was alone, in a room full of mortals already under Lilith's influence. Gwen knew she could take care of herself, but could she protect all these innocents? Lilith, if she considered them at all, thought of them as useless pawns, mere toys for her amusement. Gwen knew Lilith wouldn't hesitate to destroy any or all of them.

"What? No quick-witted banter? Are you feeling unwell *Lady* Guinevere?" The sneering insult with which she managed to imbue the word *lady* made Gwen feel slightly sick. But then, Lilith alone made her feel queasy.

"May I help you, Lady?" Gwen tried to buy time with bland politeness.

Lilith narrowed her eyes, and surveyed Gwen more closely. "There's something different about you." Her voice was so quiet Gwen almost missed her words. "Yes, Guinevere, there is something you can help me with. You can come with me to my fortress and study the spells that I have developed over the long ages. You can bring your destiny under my control."

"My destiny?" Gwen raised an eyebrow. "What do you know about my destiny?"

"Ah... so they've neglected to tell you the prophecy. But then, perhaps they don't realize it relates to you. Too bad for them.

Come, Guinevere. It's time to go, unless you want this entire room to be destroyed." She smiled evilly, licking her lips in anticipation.

Cautiously, Gwen stood, careful to keep her hands lax at her sides. "What guarantee do I have you will release them once we're gone?"

"My dear girl, these mortals have no meaning to me. Once you have bound yourself to me, their lives or deaths are of no consequence. You may make your oath contingent on their safety if you wish. It doesn't signify to me."

Gwen glanced around the room and weighed the lives of all the students and restaurant staff against her own, and knew she had no choice. She would bind herself to Lilith, but she would not live to serve her. As she confirmed her decision in her mind, she heard again the delicate melody of High Magic's acceptance and felt peace flood her soul.

Raising her right hand to form the sigil of binding, Gwen was startled to see the color drain from Lilith's face.

"Where did you get that?" Lilith screamed, her face contorted in agony. "Put it down. Get it away from me. Oh. The pain... I can't bear it."

She disappeared, leaving Gwen standing in the noisy, bustling pizza parlor with her laughing friends asking where she thought she was going?

Dazed and more than a little confused, Gwen sat down quickly. Her thoughts whirled as if she was on a merry-go-round that refused to stop. Glancing up, she saw Dylan stride through the door. His face was grimly determined until his eyes found hers. He closed his eyes and slowly exhaled, seeming to deflate. Stepping to the door, he brushed her mind with a delicate touch. *Will you join me in my office?*

Gwen managed not to jump at the intrusion of his thought, but quickly decided she'd had enough rest and relaxation for one night. *If you'll wait outside, I'll walk back with you. I need to know what just happened.*

Dylan nodded and disappeared through the door.

Quickly excusing herself from the group, Gwen laughed and said she'd had a great time, but the books were calling her. It was amazingly difficult not to run to the door and the relative safety of Dylan's company.

CHAPTER 8

"That was too close." Dylan ran his hands through his hair as they sat in the comfortable armchairs he'd conjured for the occasion. His office door was spelled against intrusion and the wards he'd placed around the room were the most powerful he knew. "She had me shielded. I didn't realize you were in trouble until her control broke. I didn't know what to expect when I walked through that door. Certainly not you sitting there with your friends as if nothing had happened."

"I've never been so frightened in my life, Dylan." Gwen's voice was quiet and controlled, but inside, she was shaking violently. "I knew I was in no danger. I mean, I can battle her sigil for sigil, plus my bracelet offers me quite a bit of protection." Gwen closed her eyes, remembering the shock of seeing all those people trapped in mid-movement. "But I also knew everyone in that room would die if I chose to fight. I had no way to protect them." She opened her eyes, took a sip of the tea Dylan had provided and lapsed into silence.

"What happened, Gwen?" The gentleness of his voice brought her back to the present.

"I'm not really sure. Lilith said something about wanting to control my destiny. She seemed surprised we didn't know what it is... something about a prophecy she thinks applies to me."

Dylan looked startled. "I wonder which prophecy she's referring to? I can't think of any that sound like you... " his voice trailed off.

"I've no idea. I don't know any of them yet. Anyway, I decided that the best thing would be to go with her, get her away from the mortals. Once I knew they were safe, that there were no others in immediate danger, I'd decided I would kill myself rather than serve her."

Dylan nodded gravely.

"Then a strange thing happened. Remember the music we heard when High Magic accepted my pledge to you and Lorenzo? Well, when I made my decision, I heard it again. I hadn't spoken aloud, but I heard that music, just the same. When I raised my hand to form the sigil of binding, Lilith freaked." As she spoke, Gwen raised her right hand again in imitation of her earlier movements. "She started screaming in pain and telling me to get *it* away from her. I've got no idea what *it* is, but I'm sure glad whatever it was forced her to leave."

Glancing at Dylan, Gwen was surprised to see him staring in awe at her upraised hand. She glanced at her hand, then back to Dylan. "What?"

A brilliant smile spread across Dylan's face. "High Magic accepted your pledge with one of its own." His face was exultant. "Look at your bracelet."

Gwen glanced again at her upraised wrist, and this time it registered. There was a new charm hanging on her bracelet. One she'd never seen before. She brought her wrist to her chest and examined the new charm more closely. Like the bracelet, it appeared to be made of silver and was also in the form of a Celtic knot, but this was a knot she didn't recognize. It was a new sigil, one that hadn't been included in the expansive collection of the Gramarye.

Gwen was dumbfounded. She stared open-mouthed at the sigil, then pleaded with Dylan with her eyes.

"Close your mouth, Gwen." Dylan had a decidedly silly grin on his face. "This is truly amazing. I've never before known High Magic to directly intercede. The bards will be writing ballads about this night."

Gwen giggled. "I keep forgetting there are still bards among the *Old Ones*. The whole idea of bards and ballads just seems so... archaic." She quickly sobered. "How do we find out what this sigil means? I'm sure it wasn't in the Gramarye."

"It wasn't," he agreed, "but I bet it is now. Shall we go take a look?"

"Can we? I mean, we're a long way from your ranch." Her face was a picture of hope weighed down by doubt.

Dylan smiled in an attempt to relieve her concern. "The Gramarye is in the overworld. We can approach it from anywhere on the planet. We just have to choose a secluded spot and work the proper sigil. Tell you what, why don't we meet in the morning at the trail head to Royal Arch? Not too many people are interested in hiking that trail in the snow. When we reach the arch, we'll open the portal."

As Gwen nodded her agreement, she realized a good night's sleep would definitely enhance her ability to study the Gramarye.

"Good night, Dylan."

She left his office and trudged toward her apartment.

~

GWEN PARKED her Jeep near the Ranger Station at Chautauqua Park early the next morning. She was looking forward to the hike up to Royal Arch, even though her friends would think she was nuts for doing it in winter. Having spent her adolescence on the ranch, she'd been doing scrambles and rock hops for as long as she could remember. This was a beautiful hike which she'd done several times over the last three summers. Besides, she was an *Old One* and Dylan would be with her.

As if conjured by her thought, Dylan appeared at her side. "Morning, Gwen. Are you ready to go?" he asked as he pulled on his gloves and prepared to tackle the trail.

Gwen nodded. "Definitely."

The two of them started up the closed access road which skirted a large meadow. In a couple of months the open space would be a sea of wild flowers, but today it was a bowl of snow. The early morning sunlight sparkled on the bowl's undisturbed surface. Here at the beginning, the road surface was hard packed, the snow crunching beneath their hiking boots, but Gwen knew that would soon change. When they reached the tree line, the boundary of the easily accessible meadow, they'd be hiking through Colorado's famous powder. She sincerely hoped it wouldn't be too deep under the trees; she hadn't thought to bring snowshoes.

They hiked in silence for nearly an hour, each lost in reverie, enjoying the freshness of the morning and the exhilaration of exercise. The trail had long ago left the gulch, and had been climbing steadily through coniferous forests. Gwen was really glad the section of trail through the gulch had been short. Wading through waist deep powder wasn't her favorite part of a winter hike. The climb through the forest, though steep, had been delightful. The snow under the trees had been shallow and manageable. The deep peace of the winter woods was a balm to her soul after last night's trauma.

As they stepped out of the trees, the sandstone arch rose before them. Gwen knew there were bigger arches in the mountains of Utah, but she loved this one. Loved the way she could frame the third flatiron through the arch's span, and the view of Boulder far below... incomparable!

"Do you know what day it is, Gwen?" Dylan's question jerked Gwen back to the present moment.

"I'm sorry? What? What day is it?" She stammered, momentarily confused. "Of course, I know. It's Saturday, February 2nd. Why?"

"Do you know the significance of the date?" Dylan pressed for more information.

"Let's see... it's Groundhog Day... but I doubt that's what you mean." Gwen closed her eyes and thought about the date. February 2nd. There was something significant about that. What was it? "Oh." she exclaimed, "It's Imbolc."

Dylan smiled. "That's right. It's Imbolc. Tell me what you know about Imbolc."

Gwen hesitated as she arranged her thoughts. "Well, it's an ancient Celtic holiday celebrating the first stirring of spring. The name literally means *in milk* and is a reference to lambing season."

"Good," he said, "but you're giving me the human definition. Go deeper."

She sighed. "You're right. That was the *linguistics student* answer. The *Old One* answer would be that Imbolc is one of the eight Arcane High Days. All eight are related to seasonal changes; four to thresholds between the seasons, four to specific positions of the sun. Imbolc gains its power from its threshold position between winter and spring. Today, it is neither winter, nor yet spring, so the barrier between this world and the overworld is particularly thin. This thinning allows more magical power to flow through the barrier."

"Wonderful." Dylan said approvingly. "Now, when did Imbolc begin?"

As she studied his face, understanding blossomed in her mind. "It began at dusk yesterday. Lilith chose to confront me at Imbolc's most powerful moment. At dusk... which is also a threshold, being neither day nor night. She was counting on the augmentation of her power to deliver me into her control. Counting on my inexperience, that I wouldn't know I could draw on that same augmented power. And she was right. I fell for it."

Dylan nodded. "But High Magic used the thinning of the barrier, along with your willingness to sacrifice yourself, to deliver you from Lilith *and* confirm you in your purpose. The physical manifestation of that unknown sigil is powerful stuff, Gwen." He finished with a whistle.

"Wait a minute," she said, "you mentioned my purpose. Did I miss something? Do you know what my purpose is now?"

Dylan shook his head. "No, but High Magic does, and unless I miss my guess, you're about to find it in the Gramarye."

Gwen closed her eyes, willed her stomach to stop turning somersaults, and clenched her hands to control their shaking. After a moment, she took a deep breath and opened her eyes. "Let's go find out."

A few minutes later, Gwen again found herself inside the great library which housed the Gramarye. To her amazement, she found that it was nothing like the last time she had visited it.

"Is it different every time you come here?" Gwen stroked the stone wall in awe.

"Different?" Dylan frowned.

"Yes, different. This is nothing like the library I was in the last time."

Gwen gazed around the large room in appreciation. It was built of massive, hand hewn stone blocks. The windows were long narrow slits, set high in the walls and were open to the sky outside. The walls held great torches in iron braces, and the bookshelves alternated with huge tapestries. The colors of the tapestries were still bright and beautiful, though their subject matter told Gwen they were ancient beyond her ability to comprehend. The fireplace crackled with warmth, but this hearth was large enough for a full grown man to walk into without troubling to lower his head. The Gramarye alone was the same, resting upon a pedestal in the center of a large wooden table; a polished jewel in a rough and ancient setting.

Dylan seemed thoughtful. "You know, in all the long centuries, I've never been in this room with another *Old One*. I always assumed everyone saw the same library, but perhaps High Magic alters the setting to suit the expectations of the seeker. How interesting." He paused, "I wonder if anything of significance will be changed because two of us are present?"

"Beats me," said Gwen. "Do you want to check the Gramarye, or shall I?"

Dylan smiled. "I think you'd better do it. High Magic gave the sigil to you. I think I'm just along for the ride on this one."

Gwen approached the ancient volume with reverence. She raised her hand to reach for it and... froze. The sigil dangling from her bracelet was glowing. She watched as the glow intensified into a narrow beam of light that sprang from the sigil and directed itself straight at the Gramarye. The Gramarye absorbed the beam of light, began to glow around the edges, and then opened ponderously. The pages rustled, and stilled as the beam vanished.

Gwen and Dylan exchanged glances over the massive book.

"Guess you were the right choice to check it out," Dylan said, his light tone at odds with the seriousness of his expression.

He walked around the table to stand beside her and they both gazed at the newly inscribed sigil, still glowing slightly around the edges.

Breaking her hand free of its arrested motion, Gwen traced the knot on the page. As her finger followed the flow of its path, the meaning and nuances of its power surged into her mind.

No wonder Lilith had fled from its presence. Not only did it offer protection, refuge, to its user (or in her case, wearer), it also commanded obedience from all magical power within its scope. Any power applied in rebellion or opposition to High Magic would be turned upon the wielder. Under the influence of this sigil, an *Old One* had two choices, to act in support of High Magic, or to use no magic.

This was a serious sigil.

Of course, it would work the same way on Gwen. She carefully considered the fact that her actions, and even her motives, would need to be above reproach while she wore this charm, or she would find herself in real trouble. Gwen shivered, and she prayed she would be up to the challenge this presented.

Dylan took his turn at tracing the sigil, then turned to Gwen with new respect. "I'm glad you're the chosen bearer. That's one hell of a responsibility you have hanging from your wrist."

"Obviously," she said dryly. "I sure hope I can handle it. I mean, I appreciate the protection, but I don't know if I can live up to the rest of its expectations."

"Gwen, High Magic is omniscient. If you've been chosen to bring this sigil to light, then you will both need it and be capable of wielding it." He put an arm around her shoulders, "This must be bound up with your purpose. Let's concentrate on finding that while we let this sigil's meaning settle into our minds."

Gwen smiled at him in gratitude. "You're right. I'm wearing it. As far as I know I can't take it off, so I must be the right person. This is just one more piece of information to absorb about myself." She moved away from the Gramarye and settled in one of the throne-like chairs beside the hearth. "Now, how does an *Old One* go about finding her purpose?"

Dylan sat in the opposing chair, hooked a leg over the arm and steepled his hands in front of his chin. "Tell me about your first burst of power. How did it manifest?"

She closed her eyes, relaxed and remembered that terrifying, yet exhilarating, moment when her world had changed. "It was like stepping into a see-through space capsule," she began, "I could look right through the walls of my apartment. I mean, everything was still there, but I could see through anything I paid attention to. Layer by layer, physical stuff just seemed to peel away in any direction I looked." Gwen opened her eyes and looked at him. "When I started to panic, I heard your voice telling me everything would be all right. As soon as I focused on your voice, the vision took me to you. It was like everything that separated us thinned into nonexistence. When I snapped back to myself, I had this map seared into my brain showing me how to get to you in the physical world."

Dylan nodded slowly, watching the flames dance on the hearth. "Well, seeking is obviously your unique gift. I've never heard of anyone's power manifesting quite like that."

"Really?" Gwen asked, "I just figured that was how all of you found each other."

"No," he laughed, "we usually mindspeak each other and show our surroundings so that the one who's traveling knows where to manifest. That's what Lorenzo and I did when he came to the ranch. I called him, explained my need, showed him my physical location, and then he teleported. He used me as his lodestone."

"Okay, so this seeking thing is unique to me. Is that my purpose?"

"No, but I'm sure it will be a necessary tool once you figure your purpose out." He tapped his index finger on his jaw, "Have you tried using it voluntarily?"

"No." Gwen answered quickly, then paused to consider her response. "Wait a minute. I did use it once, I'd almost forgotten. When I got to the ranch and realized something was wrong, I used it to find Uncle Jem and Aunt Katie. It wasn't hard, it felt completely natural — no sigils involved — I just thought about them and saw where they were."

"Great," he exclaimed, "that means it's under your control. Here's what I want you to do: relax your mind, then search for your purpose."

Gwen looked dubious, but did as she was told. A few moments later she opened her eyes and shook her head. "It's not working. I don't know what a purpose is. It's not tangible enough to seek. At least not at this stage in my development."

"That's okay, don't worry about it. We'll come at it from a different angle." Dylan frowned in concentration. "How about this? Do you think you can seek for a clue, without knowing what form the clue might take?"

Gwen thought about his suggestion for a moment. "We're in a library. How about if I seek for a book that relates to me? Or a page? That way we'd at least know if there's anything in this room."

Dylan nodded, his eyes sparkling with excitement. "That's a good thought. Give it a try."

Gwen closed her eyes, calmed her breathing and concentrated on a page of writing that was about her. Instantly she felt herself drawn into the bubble and opened her eyes. As she gazed around the room she saw several glowing dots, but one golden light was much more intense than the others, so she singled it out. At once, it was the only book in the room and she knew not only what it's cover looked like, but how it would feel beneath her fingers. She snapped back to consciousness and beamed at Dylan. "I've got it."

Jumping out of the chair, Gwen hurried across the room and stared at a towering set of shelves. Dylan followed more slowly.

"What's the matter?" he asked.

"It's up there on the top shelf," she said, puzzled, "but I don't see any ladders or anything."

Dylan tapped her on the shoulder to get her attention. She gazed at him quizzically.

"Think, Gwen," he said. "What sigil will get you what you want?"

"Oh. Right." She blushed. Concentrating on the volume she needed, Gwen drew the sigil in the air and watched as the book deposited itself in her open hands. "Magic is handy stuff," she said with a quick grin.

They moved back to the fireside, and Gwen laid the book on the table. It was a slim leather-bound volume with no title or author inscribed on the cover. Opening it, Gwen found that there was only one page she could read, the others seemed to drift just out of focus. Concentrating on that one page, she saw that it contained a short rhyme, written in an ancient Gaelic dialect. Translating as she went, she read:

> High Magic created and power awoke
> An Old One stands ready to take up her yoke.
> A new millennium reigns, and science is crowned.
> The Balance has shifted and evil abounds.
>
> At solstice and equinox and four fire feasts,
> With vision and power, the Old One seeks
> A sigil of balance by seven signs made,
> 'Twill be the undoing of the Dark now arrayed.

GWEN TURNED TO DYLAN. "Does this make sense to you?"

"Actually," he said, "it makes quite a bit of sense. The first four lines identify the *Old One*, the last four identify the quest."

"Expound on that, please, Professor," she said with a bow.

He drew a sigil in the air and a blackboard and chalk appeared in front of him. "Let's break it down line by line." He wrote the first line on the blackboard. "Pretty self-explanatory: the person is an *Old One* whose power is functioning." Gwen nodded.

"The second line starts to narrow the field." He pointed to the word *her*. "The *Old One* is a woman." She nodded again.

"The third line brings it to you." He wrote it on the board. "You're not only the only female, you're the only *Old One* who has come into her power since the new millennium began. This is definitely your quest."

"Oh," she said softly. "You're right, the rest fits our current world situation. When do you suppose this was written?"

"Long ago, and far away. Another time I'll tell you about prophecy. Right now, let's stay on task."

He wrote the final four lines on the board. "These define your task, and again, given the prominence of the word *seeks*, I'd say this is yours alone."

Gwen stared at the chalk words. "Tell me if you think I've got this right. I'm supposed to seek signs on the eight Arcane High Days which will make a sigil of balance." Dylan nodded, so she continued. "That new sigil will be the undoing of the Dark Ones?"

"That seems to cover it, from the information we have so far." He clapped his hands together to get the chalk dust off his fingers.

"Wait. There are eight Arcane High Days. This says there are seven signs. What do you suppose that means?" Gwen bit her lip as she turned her gaze on Dylan.

"I'll have to give that some thought," he admitted. "If we're finished here, let's head back to campus."

"Just a minute, when I went into seek mode a while ago, I saw several possibilities. I picked the most intense one, and got this. Let me see if I can get anything else."

Once again, Gwen entered the gelatinous bubble and saw the glowing dots around the room. She tried to concentrate on each of them individually, but none of them snapped into focus. At last she gave up and returned to her normal state.

"It's no good." Gwen tried not to let her disappointment show. "I could see the glowing dots, so I know there's stuff here that relates to me, but I couldn't get any of them to pop into focus."

Dylan patted her shoulder. "Don't worry about it. It's probably not the right time. High Magic reveals itself when it's ready, and not a moment before."

Gwen sighed, but she had plenty to think about as they left the Gramarye and made their trek back to the parking lot.

CHAPTER 9

The rest of the month of February passed in a whirlwind of activity. Gwen found herself racing from one task to the next with hardly any time to think about the quest, the prophecy, or what might be required of her on the next Arcane High Day. If she was honest with herself, she would probably have had to admit that her frantic schedule was due in large part to her unwillingness to allow herself time to think about those very topics.

It was just so daunting. It wasn't just the idea of a quest that she, and she alone, had to accomplish, though that was bad enough. No, the prophecy gave her the disturbing feeling that the peace and security of the entire world hung on her ability to complete that quest. Talk about pressure. What business did High Magic have in putting that much responsibility on her? Why, she was an infant in this sorcery stuff. There were *Old Ones* out there with tons more experience than she had, shouldn't they be the ones responsible for the fate of mankind?

These thoughts made her extremely nervous. Consequently, she drove herself so mercilessly that when she finally fell into bed at night, she was too exhausted to think.

"Hey, stranger." Kendra's words rang out merrily as she and Emily walked into the apartment Saturday morning. "What are you doing staring at a computer screen on a great day like this?"

"Yeah," agreed Emily, "you're going to blind yourself staring at that screen twenty-four seven. Come on. Get up. Come with us."

Gwen gazed bleary-eyed at the young woman pulling on her arm. "Just let me save this... " she said, then allowed herself to be hauled away from the computer and into the kitchen. Emily pushed her down onto a kitchen stool and joined Kendra in gravely looking her up and down.

"You know what she needs... " began Kendra.

"Other than a life?" interrupted Emily. Both young women giggled as Gwen narrowed her eyes and glared at them.

"She needs a spa day." Kendra finished triumphantly. "You call Andrea and see if she can bring her massage table over. I'll call Dana. She has that great paraffin dip thingy."

"Oooh. Great idea. We can all round up our cleansers and lotions and nail polishes and do facials and manicures too," Emily exclaimed with delight. "Do you think Andrea will really do massages for us?"

"Why not?" Kendra said, "she's training at Boulder College of Massage Therapy, and I hear they have to practice... and aren't allowed to charge. We'll probably be doing her a favor."

"Honestly, Gwen. Don't just sit there with your mouth hanging open. We're doing this for you. If we can't get you out to a party, we'll just have to bring the party to you." Laughing at Gwen's puzzled expression, the friends rushed for their cell phones and began making arrangements for a spur of the moment day of pampering.

More quickly than Gwen would have thought possible, the apartment was filled with young women. Andrea set up the massage table in Emily's bedroom. There was barely room to move around it, but she didn't seem to mind. The breakfast nook was crowded with paraffin dip equipment, and the living room was awash in cosmetics and nail colors. Everyone brought the snack foods they had on hand, and the kitchen was inundated with all kinds of things they knew they shouldn't eat. Evidently everyone was ready for day of indulgence.

"Okay," Andrea called, "who's up for the first massage? Remember, I'm still a beginner."

"Gwen," yelled Emily and Kendra simultaneously, and everyone else nodded their agreement. Gwen was the one who *really* needed to relax.

As she lay face down on the massage table with Andrea working out the kinks in her neck and shoulders, Gwen finally allowed herself to give in and think about the prophecy. She needed more information. She knew when to seek the first sign, but didn't have a clue where to focus her energy.

She stirred restlessly on the table, and Andrea asked if she was working too deeply. After assuring Andrea that she was doing a fabulous job, Gwen relaxed into her thoughts again. She knew how and when she was supposed to seek, just not where. How could she get more information?

Lulled by the soothing pressure of Andrea's hands, Gwen's mind eased into a trance-like state. She allowed herself to slip free of her fears and felt an idea glimmer at the edge of her consciousness.

There. That was it.

She needed to cast her power in search of information, not in the library of the Gramarye, but here in the physical world.

With that thought, she left her body in Andrea's capable hands and allowed her power to seek the data that would allow her to complete the first phase of her quest.

When Andrea woke her at the end of the massage, she was rewarded with a beatific smile from Gwen.

"That was the *best* massage in the world. Thank you so much, Andrea. You can practice on me anytime."

Gwen thoroughly enjoyed the rest of the day with her friends, and when the last of them returned to their own apartments, she gave Emily a hug.

"Thanks, roommate," she said simply, "I needed that."

Emily hugged her back. "Glad to be of service."

Monday morning found Gwen ambling across campus, kicking at the snow and humming happily to herself. She was still dreamy eyed and full of song as she let herself into Dylan's office.

"Well, well," he said, getting up from his desk, "aren't we chipper this morning?"

"I feel wonderful," Gwen grinned at him, "thanks to my roommate. She forced me to relax this weekend... and that was just what I needed."

Dylan nodded. "You have been driving yourself pretty hard since Imbolc. I figured you just needed time to process. Glad to know you're feeling better."

"About Imbolc... do you have a minute to discuss my quest?"

Dylan glanced at his watch and nodded. "I'm not due in class for another half hour. What's up?"

"I've been really nervous about finding the first sign on the vernal equinox. I mean, I know what to do, and I know when to do it, but I don't know what I'm looking for or where I should concentrate my effort. I've also been feeling like the fate of the world is resting on me..." her voice trailed off.

"I understand, Gwen," he said softly, "unfortunately, I'm not sure there's much I can do to help."

"I know, that's why I haven't brought it up before now." Gwen dropped her backpack and sat down on the wooden straight backed chair in front of his desk. "But a funny thing happened on Saturday. Em arranged for me to have a massage, and that relaxed me enough that I let my guard down. I did a quick search for a clue, but I didn't find anything."

Gwen stood up again and walked across the room to where the warded volumes were kept. "Even though I didn't find an actual clue, I was able to get past my fear of failure. To understand that when the time comes, I'll know what to do." She met Dylan's gaze straight on. "Don't get me wrong, I still have butterflies over the whole thing, but I also have a quiet assurance that I can do it, or High Magic wouldn't have asked it of me."

"Excellent!" Dylan beamed at his protege. "I can't promise I'll be with you physically at each of the Arcane High Days, but I'll be there to support you at this first one. When the time comes, you'll be great." He looked thoughtful for a moment, then cocked his head and gave her a sideways glance. "Do keep your eyes open, though. I wouldn't be surprised to find that High Magic drops a clue or two in your path between now and March 21st."

"Thanks, Dylan." Gwen grinned then checked her watch. "I'd better get to the library. Just because I'm feeling calmer doesn't

CHAPTER 10

The second week of March was now a memory, and Alban Eiler, the Arcane High Day celebrating the magical potential of the vernal equinox, was fast approaching. Though outwardly calm, Gwen was fervently wishing for some guidance as to where in the world she should seek for the first sign. So far Dylan's prediction that High Magic would give her a nudge in the right direction had not come true.

On Monday morning Gwen rushed to the library. Today she planned to spend some time doing research in the antiquities section. Most of what she needed to study would be found on microfiche, but there were a couple of original manuscripts that she was anxious to have a look at. Her thesis was coming along nicely, and Gwen hoped that today's findings might just wrap up the research portion of the process.

After checking in with Mrs. Davidson, the antiquities librarian, Gwen made her way to the study carrel that was pretty much reserved for her. She submitted her request to have hands-on time with that original manuscript, and then settled in to study the microfiche of original texts unavailable at this university.

She'd been working steadily for nearly two hours when Mrs. Davidson approached her carrel to tell her the manuscript she had requested was available.

"Thank you so much, Mrs. Davidson." Gwen straightened a pile of notes, then stood to follow the librarian. "I'm very excited about this opportunity."

"I know you are, dear," Mrs. Davidson said with a smile, "just don't forget the protocols while you're in the air-lock room. Remember the dust mask and the latex gloves. We must protect these old manuscripts, even from seemingly insignificant things like finger oil and moisture from exhalation."

Gwen assured her that she would remember all the rules and would treat the manuscript with reverential care. Then she hurried to the air-lock entrance, donned her mask and gloves, and entered the room.

This manuscript was nothing like as old as the Gramarye, but it was the oldest document she had ever handled in the human realm. A true anomaly, the document was a Shoshone manuscript, written in what appeared to be blood on a finely tanned deer hide. Scholars had argued for decades that the Shoshone people had no written language 1,500 years ago, and yet here was a manuscript written in a phonetic form of their dialect that had been carbon dated to that century.

Gwen knew the legend, but could hardly wait to read the original version with her own eyes.

As she settled down at the table, she reminded herself that this treasure had been found wrapped in a second hide in a lava tube during the construction of the road through Craters of the Moon National Monument on the Snake River plain in Idaho. She was fairly certain the discovery had happened sometime in the 1930s.

The story told of an ancient Shoshone tribe's experience with a volcanic eruption. Their attempt to understand this cataclysmic event took on a distinctly animistic cast. The legend recorded how a gigantic serpent lay coiled on a mountain top, resting. His slumber was disturbed by a powerful electrical storm. Angered by the lightning playing too close around his head, the serpent anchored his coils firmly around the mountain and prepared to strike. The problem came when he squeezed the mountain so hard in his anger that it was crushed. To his horror, the mountain erupted in red hot lava, and serpent was consumed in the liquid rock.

As Gwen studied the finely tanned leather, she became aware that a decorative drawing on the hide was pulsing and glimmering faintly. She glanced at the spot in surprise, and then gave it her full attention, quickly realizing the drawing was a tiny, intricately drawn sigil. Glancing around to make sure no one was watching, she stripped off her right glove and touched the minuscule sign...

Instantly a blank corner of the page was covered with more words in the ancient dialect. Scribbling hastily, Gwen copied the text into her notebook. When the words were safely transcribed, she glanced back at the hide and discovered that both words and sigil had disappeared.

Deciding that she was better off deciphering this particular mystery in the safety of Dylan's office, Gwen gathered up her things and left the manuscript room. Thanking Mrs. Davidson for her assistance, Gwen left the library as fast as she could empty her carrel.

Checking her watch as she ran across campus, Gwen was relieved to realize this was an open hour in Dylan's schedule. There was a good chance she would find him alone in his office. She dashed up the steps, into the linguistics building and hurried down the hall. She was panting and slightly out of breath when she came to a stop in front of his door.

"Come in, Gwen," Dylan said, chuckling as he opened his office door before she could raise her hand to knock. "You had all the subtlety of a freight train in your race across campus."

"Oh, bother subtlety." Gwen threw her books on a table and herself into a chair. "Wait 'til you see what I've found." Quickly she filled him in on her morning's work as she opened her notebook to the hastily scrawled words. Dylan looked suitably impressed as they worked out the translation together. When they were satisfied with their work, he wrote the lines on the blackboard behind his desk.

> Angered by lightning, the serpent did coil
> Bringing fire from earth's heart, a range to despoil.
> A sign he created by fire that endures,
> It waits for the Old One, she must not demur.
>
> As Light and Dark balance at Light of the Earth,
> The first sign of seven will see its rebirth.
> This sign remains hidden, awaiting her thought.
> On this day alone, by true Vision 'tis sought.

"Well," Dylan said at last, "it's pretty clear you've found a major road map to the beginning of your quest."

Gwen glowed with excitement. "I know. This not only tells me when — I mean, Alban Eiler literally means 'Light of the Earth' — but how to find it, and more importantly *where* to look. It even tells me what I'm searching for."

Dylan looked skeptical. "You really got that much out of these lines?"

"Of course." She tried not to gloat as she explained her reasoning. "It was on a manuscript about the Shoshone legend of how Craters of the Moon National Monument was formed... so that's where, and the sigil will be *fire that endures*. I'm guessing cooled lava fits that description."

Nodding slowly, Dylan reread the rhyme. "I agree. The where — which is the most important piece of the puzzle — is undoubtedly in the lava flow now known as Craters of the Moon. It only makes sense that the sign would be formed of that substance as well."

Dylan offered Gwen his right hand in a solemn handshake. "Congratulations, my dear."

As soon as Gwen put her hand in his, Dylan dropped the sober demeanor and gave her a toothy grin. "I guess we know what we'll be doing Thursday night."

BY THE TIME Alban Eiler arrived, Gwen was an emotional basket case. Now that she knew what was supposed to happen, she was so excited she could hardly wait. Even her friends remarked that she was like a six-year-old on Christmas morning.

Emily and Kendra were positive there was a new guy in her life. They were convinced Gwen was keeping secrets, holding out on them. Gwen kept telling everyone she was excited about a new legend she had discovered. After all, it was a big honor to be the first one on campus to decipher a cryptic artifact. That story satisfied her friends in the linguistics department, but her roommate didn't buy it.

"Come on, Gwen." Emily flopped on the couch, eyeing Gwen intently. Something was up, and she was determined to figure it out. "Nobody in their right mind gets this excited over a piece of paper. What's going on with you? Give."

"Who said I was in my *right mind*?" Gwen replied with a laugh. "Ease up. You've been after me for weeks to cheer up. I'm cheerful. What more do you want?"

Emily scowled at her and flounced out of the apartment. If Gwen didn't want to tell her about this new guy, she didn't want to hear it... at least not right now. She'd worm it out of her later.

Gwen glanced at her watch for the thousandth time that day. Time was creeping by. She felt as if the appointed hour would never arrive. The tension was almost palpable. She wanted to get this show on the road. Success or failure... she wasn't sure it mattered. She just wanted it to be done. Conclusion was the only antidote for this knot in the pit of her stomach.

She and Dylan had decided the optimal time to seek the sign would be dusk. Alban Eiler, or the vernal equinox, marked the spring day when the hours of light exactly balanced the hours of darkness. The *Old Ones* would approach the quest at the pivotal moment — the instant between light and dark — on one of the two perfectly balanced days of the year.

In order to avoid gossip, they had agreed to teleport to Dylan's office. Once inside, Dylan would set wards to protect them from mortal or magical interruptions.

Gwen was nervous about teleporting across campus. She had made a couple of trial runs in the middle of the night, just to reassure herself that she could actually do it, but this was different. The timing needed to be perfect. There very little margin for error in getting to Dylan's office, and even less when it came to actually recovering the sign.

As the agreed upon hour approached, Gwen closed her bedroom door, turned her stereo on and arranged her pillows to simulate a sleeping body. Her preparations made, she took a deep breath, visualized a corner of open space in Dylan's office, and willed herself to *be* there. For just a breath she felt panic as her physical being compressed to a psychic echo of thought... but then the relief of expansion burst in, leaving no room for any other emotion.

"Wow." Gwen spoke aloud, needing the confirmation of hearing her own voice. "What an exhilarating ride. Will I ever get used to the sensation?"

Dylan, who had popped in a moment before her, clapped a hand on her back. "It gets easier, but it's still a rush for me. And I've been doing it a *long* time." He ran a hand through his hair as he glanced at the clock. "Let's get the wards in place. We haven't got a lot of extra time."

Working quickly and efficiently, they soon had the room secured and the furniture arranged to suit their needs. Gwen gazed at Dylan with satisfaction. "Whether I succeed or fail, I'm as ready as I know how to be. Wish me luck?"

"You know I do." Dylan gazed solemnly into her eyes. "I'll maintain a light link with your mind. That way I should be able to follow you when you teleport to retrieve the sign. I don't anticipate any interference from Lilith, but I'll stay as close as I can, just in case."

Gwen nodded her understanding. Her excitement and nerves were rapidly turning to fear, and she didn't trust herself to speak. Dylan seemed to understand. He motioned her to a chair and they took their places as the threshold moment of *not-day-not-night* descended on them. Gwen closed her eyes, entered the gelatinous bubble of magical power, and threw her consciousness in search of the first sign.

What a fascinating experience. Wherever she turned her attention, the physical realm dissolved in layers. The longer she rested her thought on a spot, the further she could see in that direction. There were no physical barriers that could hold back her sight. Through force of will she pulled her sense of wonder under control and began to systematically peel away the distance to the Snake River plain in Idaho, where she knew Craters of the Moon would be found. As the barriers to her sight fell away she became aware of a soft golden glow that pulsed faintly and pulled her forward. The closer she came, the stronger it pulsed, until she located it in an underground lava tube near the Great Rift.

Without bothering to snap back to normal consciousness, Gwen teleported to the site.

This time the compression-panic threatened to overwhelm her. She had never attempted this great a distance before, and she had never initiated teleportation from within the gelatinous bubble of her unique power. Gwen had nearly reached the limit of her sanity when the expansion-relief washed over her in soothing waves.

She had survived.

Dylan arrived a split second later and formed a sigil, bathing their immediate vicinity in light. Blackness surrounded their little oasis, swallowing the edges of light and threatening to devour the rest. The tube was about eight feet wide and seven feet high in the center, which was where they stood. Formed as the outside edges of a lava stream cooled around the still moving core of molten lava, the flow had eventually ceased and the last of the lava had spilled out onto the plain, leaving this tunnel behind. It seemed to stretch away to infinity in the direction of its flow.

Despite the light that Dylan had conjured, Gwen could still see the golden, pulsating light that had drawn her to this place. Reaching out her hand, she touched the center of the glow and a shining black fragment came loose in her right hand.

Her eyes alight with wonder, Gwen turned to show the sigil to Dylan. "What should I do with it?"

Dylan gazed at the sign in awed silence, before admitting he didn't have a clue. He watched as Gwen transferred the lava to her left hand and yelled as realization struck him.

"Sorry," he said softly, as the echoes of his cry died away, "I didn't mean to startle you. Try bringing it in contact with the protection sigil High Magic gave you." When she stared blankly at him, he tried again. "On your bracelet. Put it next to the sigil on your bracelet."

"Oh." Gwen's eyes widened in surprise, but she did as he suggested. Immediately the lava fragment dwindled in size and attached itself to a link on the bracelet. Now the sign appeared to be no more than an oddly shaped black charm. "I guess that answers the question of where I'm supposed to keep the signs until I have them all assembled. Did you know that would happen?"

"Nope," Dylan answered honestly, "but when you traded hands, I saw that you *could* put the two signs together, and I figured it wouldn't hurt to try." He grinned at her, "Congratulations, Gwen. You've just successfully completed the first task of your quest."

He hugged her and lifted her off her feet, forgetting they were standing in a lava tube. She squealed as her head hit the top of the tube and he set her down quickly.

"How about we get out of here and find someplace more appropriate to celebrate?" Gwen rubbed the top of her head, where a tender knot was forming.

Dylan traced a healing sigil over the knot, and the two of them dissolved into relieved laughter.

How do Old Ones celebrate? That was the question uppermost in Gwen's mind as she and Dylan arrived back in his office. The answer soon became clear. They plan a party.

Dylan removed the wards, held a quick mindspeech conversation with Lorenzo, and described an obscure sigil to Gwen. He asked her to perform the sigil so that he knew she would be able to get to their destination another time. Obligingly, Gwen drew the sigil in the air of his office and they stepped through the resulting door into the overworld.

That was how Gwen came to be standing in a forest glade with seven other *Old Ones*. Lorenzo and Dylan she knew. Now she had the opportunity to meet five more *Old Ones*.

"We thought you'd like to know a few more of our family before we all get together at Beltane." Lorenzo took her arm and proceeded to make the introductions. "This is Ingrid." He indicated a tall Scandinavian woman who stepped forward to give Gwen a hug.

"Blessings on you, Gwen, we are so pleased with your accomplishment." Ingrid smiled and Gwen was reminded of the many tales of Valkyries she had studied.

Gwen was alternately saluted and hugged by each of the remaining *Old Ones*: Omar, a distinguished looking Arab man; Mei, a petite and lovely Chinese woman; Kunto, an African man with a forbidding appearance; and finally, Phoebe, the living incarnation of a Greek goddess. Each of them welcomed her to the extended family and congratulated her on the successful completion of the first step on her quest.

The glade where the *Old Ones* stood was surrounded by linden and laurel trees. Though the air was still, Gwen could smell the delicious fragrance of their blossoms. The grass in the clearing was soft and springy, inviting her feet to walk its soft carpet. In the center of the open space stood a majestic spreading oak. Under its protecting branches stood a table laden with food. The aroma that wafted toward her was enticing, and her stomach grumbled its desire to become better acquainted with that smell. Mei took Gwen's hand and led her toward the feast.

"You must be starving," Mei said gently, "I bet you didn't eat a thing in anticipation of your quest."

Gwen blushed and nodded. Mei smiled in understanding. "Well, now is the time to rest and refresh. Remember, it is always light in the overworld, and no time will have passed when you return to your own place in the mortal realm."

"This is where we come to relax and replenish our souls." Kunto joined them at the table, carrying a large platter of food. "Be at ease among us."

With that, Gwen relaxed and found that she truly enjoyed the company of her fellow *Old Ones*. Chairs littered the shaded area under the oak, and the *Old Ones* settled in them in knots of twos and threes. As she gazed around the gathering an hour or so later, she was struck by the cultural diversity which the *Old Ones* represented.

"Excuse me." Gwen was a little embarrassed as the group fell silent, every eye on her face. "Please forgive my ignorance, and I mean no disrespect, but I thought the sigils we use were Celtic, which would make *us* Celtic."

The silence lengthened, though Gwen was sure she saw amused glances being exchanged. Finally, Omar spoke, his bass voice booming through the stillness. "*Old Ones* are of every race... and no race. Ultimately, we are a people apart."

"The phrase *Old One* is from the first language," said Phoebe, "a tongue so ancient no record of it remains, save that single name. And as for our sigils…"

"There is a reason the mortal realm associates our sigils so strongly with the Celts." Ingrid said, taking up the tale.

"Yes," agreed Lorenzo, "the Celts simply refused to forget us."

"They have always been a most stubborn race." Kunto scowled, as if remembering the antics of a troublesome child. "We sought to remove ourselves from the notice of man, and they responded by immortalizing every scrap of information they could find in story and song."

"Why, they even went so far," continued Mei, "as to commemorate our sigils by rendering them in jewelry and art."

"Our magic spells became decoration for their books, their homes and their bodies." Omar declared with a more than a hint of exasperation.

"Finally, we did fade into legend," Dylan said with an air of finality, "but, because of their determination to hold onto us, the most accurate traces that remain among mortals have a decidedly Celtic flair."

After that, the conversation turned to individual memories... stories of each of their first months as *Old Ones*. Gwen was amazed to find that each of them had been given a task or quest to complete, as well as unique abilities which had allowed them to succeed. She was so happy in their company, that she truly didn't want to return to campus. However, when Dylan finally suggested that it was time to return, Gwen realized she was bone tired, and would greatly appreciate her bed.

As she said her good-byes to her new friends, Gwen was reminded that all the *Old Ones* would gather for the festival of Beltane. She would be among them again at the end of April.

Back in Dylan's office at last, Gwen thanked him warmly for his unfailing support and for arranging her first *Old One* celebration. Then, exhausted but very happy, she teleported to her warm, cozy bed.

CHAPTER 11

The next afternoon Gwen finished her research for the week and returned to her apartment. As she was retrieving her mail from the box in the lobby, Emily entered the building.

"Hallelujah. Spring Break has arrived." Noticing the shocked expression on Gwen's face, Emily rolled her eyes. "Don't tell me you've been so buried in your books you forgot we have a whole week off? Gwen. You've got to reenter the real world."

"No," Gwen lied, "I know it's Spring Break. You just surprised me with your shouting."

Chiding herself for losing track of the academic calendar, Gwen followed Emily to their apartment. Once inside, she sorted through the mail as she tried to concentrate on Emily's excited chatter.

"So where are you going for Spring Break? I mean, this is the *big* one. Spring Break of our senior year."

"Oh, I don't have any... " Gwen began, then stopped and stared at the letter in her hand.

Emily looked up, "What is it, Gwen?"

"It's a reply from one of the grad schools I applied to." Gwen's fingers tightened on the unopened envelope. Her pulse raced and her hands shook. "Oh, I don't think I can do this. You open it, Emily." She thrust the offending envelope into Emily's hand.

Emily glanced at the crest on the envelope and read, *Office of Graduate Studies, Portland State University*. "Ooooh, this is the one you really want, isn't it?" Noticing the pallor of Gwen's face, Emily hurried to find the letter opener. "Okay, here goes."

Gwen closed her eyes and listened intently as Emily sliced the envelope open and quickly scanned the contents.

"You did it." Emily jumped up and down, waving the sheet of paper in the air. "You're in. All you have to do is complete your degree here at CU and you're off to Portland, Oregon."

Gwen screamed with delight. She and Emily danced around the living room for a few wild minutes, and then collapsed on the couch.

"*Now* I have plans for Spring Break." Gwen announced, eyes shining with excitement. "I'm going to drive to Portland and explore the university. I haven't been to Portland since I was a child. I applied on the strength of their catalog. Now that I've been accepted, I want to see the campus for myself."

"That's a great idea," Emily agreed, "after all, you might get accepted to another school; you'll want to make the right choice."

After a hurried consultation with Dylan, Gwen spent the evening packing, calling her aunt and uncle to let them know her plans, and studying the road map to determine the best route between

Boulder and Portland. She knew it would be a two-day drive, which was definitely the longest solo trip she'd ever made. That would get her into Portland by Sunday evening. Gwen would be walking around on her new campus Monday morning. Once there, she would determine her plans on a daily basis. As long as she was headed home by the following Saturday, she'd be in great shape.

Just imagine, she thought dreamily, *a whole week to wander around campus and get reacquainted with Portland. This is going to be a blast.*

Bright and early the next morning Gwen loaded her luggage in the Jeep and set off on her cross-country adventure. The early spring day was gorgeous; crisp, with a cloudless blue sky. The forecast was for clear weather, so even though she was prepared for a spring blizzard, she didn't expect to have any excitement of that nature on her drive.

She'd decided to drive the Diagonal to Longmont and then catch US 287 north to Wyoming where she'd catch Interstate 80 west. It would probably be faster to go east to I-25 and then north to its intersection with I-80, but she was too anxious to head *west* to start her journey by driving *east*. Besides, this was her adventure. She didn't have to be sensible if she didn't want to.

Late afternoon found Gwen driving through the mountains of Utah. While she wasn't exactly *excited* by the journey anymore, she was enjoying the peace and solitude of the drive. She didn't know how long it had been since she'd had an excuse to listen to her favorite CDs for hours on end, not to mention the audio books Kendra had lent her. Those was for emergencies — in case she got tired of the CDs and was in an area where the radio reception was intermittent.

Her destination this evening was Tremonton, Utah. Gwen thought she could probably make it all the way to Twin Falls,

Idaho, but Tremonton was basically the half-way point of her journey and she decided she didn't need to push herself. Besides, southern Idaho along I-84 contained some pretty empty stretches of highway. She figured she'd be safer, and a lot more comfortable, making that drive during daylight hours.

Driving north on I-15, Gwen enjoyed seeing the Great Salt Lake. Giving in to a restless desire to stretch her legs, she pulled off the highway at Willard Bay State Park. She had stopped for a burger at a fast food restaurant in Ogden not too long ago, but had eaten hurriedly, anxious to be on the road again. Now she wanted to take a few minutes to stretch and enjoy the scenery, without the need to fill either the car's tank or her own stomach.

Gwen parked in a lot, locked the car, and walked down to the white sandy beach of the bay. She walked along the water's edge, enjoying the cool of the evening air against her face, very grateful for the warmth of the fleece jacket that protected her torso. The light of the setting sun was fading as she came to an area that was blocked from view of the parking area by a small stand of scrub trees.

A frisson of anxiety halted her wandering. Extending her senses, she turned to scan the trees... and saw two men leaning casually against a picnic table. Behind them, a third person stood shrouded in shadow. The dimming light made it difficult to distinguish their faces, but she had the odd feeling she should know them.

Straightening her back, and taking her hands out of her pockets, she stared directly at them. "Do I know you?"

The taller man chuckled ominously. "You should, if you've done your homework properly."

"We're *cousins*, so to speak," said the shorter man. He was soft around the middle and had a doughy, unhealthy caste to his face.

"You know, the dark sheep of the family."

The broad hint was sufficient. Gwen placed them as Lilith's followers. Dark *Old Ones* who had joined her — whether willingly or by seduction was of little consequence — in her plots to subvert High Magic and enslave mankind.

"What can I do for you, then... Cousins?" Gwen watched them warily, unsure of their intentions.

"You can come along quietly, like a nice little girl," said the taller *Old One*. "Our mistress desires your company."

He moved his hand to invoke a sigil as Gwen raised her right hand, bringing High Magic's protective charm into view. The *Old One* caught his breath and winced, but continued to draw his sigil in the air. Gwen watched in fascinated horror as the strands of magic he was attempting to weave buckled and fought his control. His breathing became labored and he sweated profusely, but he refused to relinquish the sigil. The harder he tried to direct its energy, the wilder and stronger the strands of magic became until they broke free... and destroyed him in their backlash.

The doughy faced *Old One* tore his eyes away from the charred remains of his partner and stared at Gwen in shock. She could see him weighing his options, and then, as she continued to hold the sigil between them, he disappeared.

"High Magic protects you well, child." A familiar voice spoke from the shadows. "I will miss Samuel, and Luther may well wish he had perished with his friend before I finish disciplining him for his hasty retreat." Lilith laughed, but there was no humor in the sound.

"You cannot harm me, Lilith." Gwen's voice was quiet, but assured. "There are no hostages to my good conduct this time.

Your thugs have failed, so you'd just as well follow Luther."

"Failed?" she cried, "oh, no, my dear. Samuel did not fail. I required information about that sigil you wear, and he provided it to me. He followed my instructions admirably. If only Luther had done his part as well." She sighed. "I don't suppose you'd like to tell me what the Gramarye taught you about that charm?"

Gwen smiled. "No, but you're welcome to visit the Gramarye and learn its properties for yourself." She paused, gave a little frown, and then continued. "Oh. Wait. I forgot. You gave up that right when you rebelled against High Magic."

Lilith's face went white with rage, but she tightened her lips and said nothing.

Gwen smiled cheerfully at Lilith. "Sorry. Guess you're out of luck!"

After a moment, Lilith shrugged. "Ah well, I expected no more. Experiments are so time consuming, and," she nudged Samuel's remains with her toe, "costly. Fortunately, they aren't costs I have to pay."

"Do your followers know how expensive it is to be in your little circle?" Gwen watched Lilith closely. The older woman smiled cruelly, but made no reply. "By the way, Lilith," Gwen said as a new thought struck her, "how did you manage to find me? This was hardly a planned stop on my itinerary."

"Let's just say you have your little secrets and I have mine." Lilith circled Gwen like a cat circling an injured bird, then drew herself up straight. "Until we meet again, child." She vanished, leaving Samuel's corpse where it lay.

Gwen snorted, surprised Lilith hadn't produced a puff of smoke. It certainly would have fit the melodramatic exit. Looking with disgust at the smoldering remains on the beach, Gwen traced a

CHAPTER 12

*M*onday morning found Gwen strolling the grounds of Portland State University. She'd arrived at her downtown hotel the night before, tired, but very pleased with herself. After a restful night, she'd enjoyed a hot breakfast of waffles, bacon, and scrambled eggs, compliments of the hotel, and then set out to explore the PSU campus.

Because it was situated in the heart of a major metropolitan city, Portland State was much more compact than the University of Colorado's Boulder campus. However, it made wonderful use of a long central core of park, reminding Gwen strongly of the Pearl Street Mall in Boulder. Both were essentially city streets which had been closed to traffic and landscaped — one as a walking mall, the other as a campus park complete with mini amphitheater. The large campus buildings on either side of the park had banks of windows looking out on the green space, fostering the illusion of expansive campus lawns.

Gwen was enchanted with the climate of the Willamette Valley in general and Portland State in particular. It was only March, but already the grass was emerald green and flowers bloomed everywhere she looked. Coming from Colorado, where spring was still lazily stretching in an attempt to awaken, Gwen felt like she had leapt forward in time. The air was still cool here, but it was soft with fragrance and held the allure of verdant lushness. Even here in the center of a bustling city, the atmosphere alone was enough to seduce her senses. She was in love, and knew that having seen this campus in spring, no other university would be a viable option.

The compactness of the campus, coupled with the close proximity of downtown's cultural attractions excited her. If she could only find an apartment nearby, she'd hardly need to use her car. Between the bus system and the light rail, everything she needed was easily accessible.

Gwen wandered into the building which housed the admissions office, and found that very few of the staff were present. As she had anticipated, Portland State was also on spring break. Surprisingly, she found it didn't really matter. She hadn't come to interview professors, or query existing students.

She had come to allow the campus to speak to her, and it had done so exuberantly in the first few moments of her stroll. The campus welcomed her, from its stately trees, to the statues adorning its walks, and Gwen responded with a deep sense of gratitude. She felt at ease, almost at home, on the campus.

She spent much of the afternoon sitting under a tree in a park beside the Willamette River. With maps and notebooks at hand, she carefully planned her remaining days in the area. She wanted to see if she could find the home she had grown up in. She remembered the address, so with the help of a detailed map locating it shouldn't prove too difficult.

Another deep desire was to find an apartment near the university. She wouldn't be ready to move until mid-May, but she wanted to choose her location while she was able to inspect her choices. That goal might prove to be a challenge.

Finally, she wanted to take a day and drive to the coast. Gwen remembered a wonderful condominium that her parents had taken her to in Cannon Beach. She hoped to be able to find it as well.

With her week's itinerary firmly in mind, Gwen went in search of dinner and then treated herself to a movie in a lovely old theater.

AS SHE HAD EXPECTED, finding her childhood home was not diffi-cult. Gwen sat in her parked car, staring at the lovely old home. She was torn. Part of her wanted to run up the walk and ring the doorbell, but her logical side kept her rooted to the car seat. There was no point. When the door opened, it would not be her mother standing there.

Shaking herself, Gwen reached for the ignition and then paused again. The child inside wasn't quite ready to leave the neigh-borhood.

I don't suppose there's anything wrong with taking a walk down the street, her child-self thought.

Don't kid yourself, her rational mind responded, *if you get out of this car, you'll end up on that porch.*

As she hesitated, a young girl ran around the side of the house and down the front walk. When she reached the street, she noticed Gwen sitting in her car watching her progress. The girl backed up a step, then turned and bolted to the house. A moment later, the child returned, accompanied by a slim young woman.

Great, she thought as the young mother approached the Jeep. *I've been busted. She probably thinks I'm a criminal.*

"May I help you?" The young woman leaned down to peer in the passenger-side window.

"I'm sorry," Gwen said with a smile, "I didn't mean to startle your daughter. I've just been sitting here remembering. I grew up in that house."

"Oh, I see." The woman hesitated, then smiled shyly. "Would you like to come inside?"

Gwen glanced from the young mother to the child hugging the front porch post and shook her head. "Thank you, but no. It's your home now, and it's better that I leave the past in the past." As she spoke, her heart was flooded with a sense of peace. She smiled at the woman and calmly drove away.

The search for the perfect apartment wasn't quite as easy. She spent all of Tuesday afternoon, as well as Wednesday morning, going from apartment complex to apartment complex. None of them was quite what she was looking for. Some were too far from campus — she really wanted to be in walking distance. Some were close enough, but lacked the peace and dignity she desired. A couple of them were just perfect, but the rents were outrageous.

Just when she was ready to cry with frustration, she found the perfect building. It was a small complex — two stories with a parking garage below. Built around a central courtyard, the building was ivy covered brick. The courtyard was visible from the street, but was gated and required an electronic key to enter. The complex was only two blocks from campus, and Gwen couldn't imagine how she had missed it in her earlier search.

"Come in, Miss Vaughan." The manager was a stout little lady dressed in a tweed skirt, white blouse and charcoal gray cardigan. "Tell me what you're hoping for, and I'll see if I can be of assistance."

Gwen sat down in an upholstered armchair and told Mrs. Gresham she would soon be a graduate student at PSU and needed a one bedroom apartment. Her only specific requirement was her need for proper wiring for computer access.

"There's no problem with that, my dear." Mrs. Gresham waved the consideration away. "We were renovated several years ago to make sure our tenants could join the information age, if they so chose." She smiled at Gwen. "We have no vacancies at the moment. However," she hurried on as disappointment flooded Gwen's face, "I agreed to see you because you said you didn't need to move in right away."

"You have an apartment opening up?" Gwen asked excitedly.

"Yes, indeed." Mrs. Gresham beamed, her plump cheeks dimpling. "Professor Lockridge, in 3B, is leaving at the end of the term. He has accepted an appointment back east. He assured me that the unit will be empty by May 25th. We'll need a week or so to clean and make any necessary repairs, but I think you could expect to move in the first week of June. Would that fit your time table?"

"Oh, Mrs. Gresham, that would be perfect." Gwen sighed, she was going to get her apartment. "How big is 3B?"

"Well, that may be a problem. It's a two bedroom unit, and you've requested a one bedroom."

"I think I can live with that. Let's discuss the details."

An hour later, after finalizing the terms of their agreement — including parking privileges, pet policies and financial arrangements — Gwen left the building with a signed lease and a detailed floor plan of her new home. A very productive day, indeed.

That evening she called Dylan to share her delight at finding the perfect apartment. "I just can't believe everything is falling into place so perfectly." she told him. "I love the campus, I've found a fabulous place to live, and I've even managed to close the door on my childhood home. It's been a wonderful trip."

"That's great, Gwen," he said, pleased to hear her sounding so happy. "You've really accomplished a lot in three days. What are you planning for the rest of your break?"

"I'm driving out to the coast tomorrow. I really want to see Cannon Beach again. I remember lots of fun weekends there with my parents." As an afterthought she added, "I don't know where I'll stay, but I'm sure I'll find something."

Dylan was very quiet on the other end of the phone line. When he spoke again, his voice was hesitant. "I don't know whether I should mention this or not... you seem to be letting go of the past so nicely... "

"Tell me," she urged, "whatever it is, I'm sure I'll be fine."

"Well, it's just that, uh, well, I was the one who set up the trust for you. I chose what assets to liquidate, and what to hold onto... "

"You held onto some of my parents assets?" Gwen hardly dared to breathe, she'd never dreamed any of her parents' possessions might still exist. "Like what?"

"Like their condo in Cannon Beach," he replied. "It was pretty liquid without being sold. I was able to place it in a rental pool. The rents have paid for its management and maintenance, and have even added a bit to the balance in your trust."

"Wait a minute," she cried, "are you saying I own a condo in Cannon Beach?"

"That's what I'm saying. Let me give you the number for the management company. It's very short notice, but it's possible you might be able to stay there tomorrow night."

Gwen called the management company as soon as she finished talking to Dylan. Identifying herself as the owner of the condo, she asked about its status for the next few nights. She was told that it was occupied at the moment, and that it was reserved for all of next week, beginning Saturday afternoon. However, it would be vacant from 11:00 am tomorrow until 3:00 pm Saturday. Gwen had to suppress a squeal of delight as she tried to calmly make arrangements to use it herself during the short vacant period.

"I'm going to Cannon Beach," she said to herself after hanging up the phone, "and I'm going to stay in my very own condo." She sat down abruptly, her eyes filling with tears. "Thanks, Mom and Dad," she whispered, "and thank you, Dylan, for saving it for me."

CHAPTER 13

*C*annon Beach was as wonderful as she remembered. A crisp, clean little community, with an economy driven by tourism, the town had managed to resist the temptation to devolve into gimmickry and tawdry shops. Its natural attractions were wide white beaches, and Haystack Rock, a towering, barnacle-encrusted monument to the sea.

As a child, Gwen had loved exploring the tidal pools at the Rock's base. Her parents, sensitive to the Rock's fragile ecosystem, had never allowed her to climb on it or remove any of the numerous marine creatures from its tide pools. Probably because of their concern for the Rock and its inhabitants, Gwen loved it fiercely. She found, now that she was here, she could hardly wait to get a glimpse of her old friend.

Curbing her excitement a little while longer, Gwen parked the Jeep and went into the management office to retrieve the key to her condo. After exchanging pleasantries and filling out the requisite paperwork, Gwen took her key and drove to the condo.

The condo was just as she remembered it: situated on the fourth floor, with a balcony overlooking the ocean. Standing on that balcony, she was awed by the view… nothing between her and the horizon but the white beach and the sweep of the sea. Looking just a little to her left she could see Haystack Rock rising from the water at the edge of the sand. The sound of the surf throwing itself upon the shoreline was a siren's call to her soul.

Hurriedly she returned to her bedroom and, rummaging through her luggage, found a pair of sweat pants, sandals and a windbreaker. After carefully rolling the sweat pants to her knees, she made her way to the beach for a long-anticipated stroll.

Gwen reveled in her solitary walk on the beach. She was not alone, but neither was the beach crowded. No one approached her, and the roar of the waves drowned out the voices of any people who happened past her.

She had forgotten how deceptive distances could be on a beach. It took much longer than she had expected to reach the tidal pools at the base of Haystack Rock. But once there, Gwen gave in to temptation and removed her sandals. The sand varied from hard as concrete where the waves had pounded it to soft and squishy where it had been lightly deposited between the rocks of the tidal pools.

Stepping carefully to avoid treading on living creatures, she wandered around the tidal pools… and through her memories. The allure of the Rock and its pools remained strong, and Gwen, totally immersed in her fascination with the varied inhabitants of the sun-warmed shallow pools, almost missed the fact that someone had called her name.

She glanced up, and found herself facing Lorenzo Santini.

"Lorenzo." Gwen shaded her eyes with her hand as she gazed at the *Old One* in amazement. "What on earth are you doing here?"

"Spying on you." He grinned until suspicion narrowed her eyes and he changed his tack. "Actually, I came to keep you company. I thought you might like someone to talk to. Someone who isn't responsible for your training." He paused and watched her face intently. "But, if I'm intruding on your vacation, I'll leave immediately."

He raised his hand to trace a sigil, but Gwen reached out and caught it.

"No, please don't go." She hesitated, then laughed apologetically. "I seem to be getting paranoid. I didn't mean to question your motives." She realized she was still holding his hand and dropped it quickly. Lowering her eyes and wiping her hands on her sweats, she said, "I'd love to have some company, especially someone I can talk to freely."

Lorenzo smiled at her quick release of his hand. "I remember. It's difficult at first, trying to decide what you can say, what must remain secret."

"That's it exactly," Gwen agreed enthusiastically. "I used to tell Emily and Kendra everything... now I find myself avoiding conversations with them just so I don't have to worry about what I might let slip."

"It does get easier," he assured her, "but mainly because we make friends among our own. You haven't had time to make those connections; I wanted to make sure you weren't feeling isolated."

"Dylan's been wonderful," she said hurriedly, "but it would be nice to have someone else to talk to ... " She glanced shyly into his eyes, and received a physical jolt. For just an instant she thought she had seen raw passion shining in his eyes, but it disappeared so quickly... she must have been mistaken. Lorenzo thought of her as a child, just as Dylan did.

No matter, Gwen was happy to have an excuse to be near him. Lorenzo Santini was the most attractive man she had ever met... mortal or *Old One*. Not the most handsome, perhaps, nut definitely the one who drew her eyes. He embodied pure animal magnetism as far as she was concerned.

A shiver ran down her spine. She had to pull herself together, to stop imagining things that didn't exist. He was offering her friendship. Nothing more.

Lorenzo must have seen her shiver, he reached to pull her into the shelter of his arms. Correctly interpreting the intent of his movement, Gwen stepped quickly away... and into the tide pool she had been studying.

Thrown off balance, she was definitely falling when Lorenzo caught her in his arms; the very thing she had been trying to avoid.

He pulled her a few paces down the beach and settled her on the hard packed sand. "Are you all right?" he asked, eyes full of concern.

"I'm fine," she assured him, "just a little embarrassed by my clumsiness."

"You're never clumsy, Gwen." He gazed into her eyes, and then quickly broke contact, both physical and psychic. Flushing slightly, he turned and glanced down the beach toward the public access.

"Would you like to walk back into town? Maybe have some pizza?"

She studied him speculatively and slipped her sandals back on before answering. "I'd love to wander around town a bit. But if you don't mind, I can have pizza anytime. It's been years since I've had clam chowder."

"Clam chowder, it is," he agreed. "And call me Renzo."

Later that afternoon Renzo and Gwen sat at a table looking out at the Pacific Ocean while they waited for bowls of clam chowder to arrive. They had meandered through shops and galleries 'til Gwen's feet and legs ached. When they finally chose this small seafood restaurant, she was delighted to do nothing more strenuous than sit and gaze at the ocean.

It had been a magical day — without the need of sigils.

Gwen loved spending time with Renzo. Not only did she find him physically attractive, but his personality and warm humor delighted her as well. They hadn't shared any deep philosophical discussions; they had simply enjoyed the novelty of looking in shop windows, browsing counters laden with trinkets, and admiring the handiwork of obviously talented artisans. They had discovered areas where their tastes were very similar, and aspects of their personalities that jarred wildly.

In short, they had enjoyed a day of getting to know each other.

Glancing across the table at him now, it occurred to Gwen that she had never asked how he came to be in Cannon Beach.

"Renzo, did you come here looking for me, or was today simply a coincidence?"

"I don't believe in coincidences," he said, the light in his eyes dancing merrily. "No, I was on a mission. I came to find you, and if you had preferred solitude, I'd be back home in California right now."

"But how did you know where to find me?"

"I asked Dylan, of course."

"Well, that certainly explains it. He always knows where I am whether I report in or not, and I've been reporting in regularly."

Her eyes clouded, "Did he tell you about my encounter with Lilith in Utah?"

His reaction startled her. The color drained from his face and then built again as the red of anger flushed his features. "No," he said, "he neglected to mention that you'd been in danger."

She reached across the table and took his hand. "I'm fine, Renzo. I truly wasn't in danger." Speaking quietly and calmly, she told him about her two most recent visits from Lilith, as well as the new sigil High Magic had provided for her protection. She watched in relief as the fierce expression left his face and his color returned to normal. Without relinquishing her hand, he touched the silver sigil that adorned her wrist.

"I knew you were special the moment I saw you as an adult... a newly awakened *Old One* calmly facing down the Queen of Darkness. But I had no idea how special. High Magic never offers us protection. If we're killed in its service, we die - and another eventually appears to take up our duties." He raised his eyes to hers and she felt as if she might drown in the emotion she saw swirling there.

"You amaze me, Guinevere." He said it so quietly she almost missed it, the throbbing of her own pulse was so loud in her ears.

The intensely intimate moment was shattered by the waitress setting bowls of chowder in front of them. They started, dropped their clasped hands and grinned guiltily at the young woman as she asked if they needed anything else. They thanked her hastily, and avoiding each other's eyes, began to eat in silence. Lost in their own confused thoughts, they seemed uncertain how to restart the conversation.

However, the unexpected intimacy dissipated and soon they were chatting about inane and unimportant topics. Gwen laughed at his jokes and paid rapt attention to his stories, yet deep inside she knew that when they went their separate ways, it would be those few unguarded moments that would sustain her. She had experienced real magic here tonight — a magic unfettered by sigils or strands of power — and she would treasure its memory forever.

"I can't believe it's Friday." Gwen laughed as Renzo helped her into a little red Mustang the next morning. "The last day of my Oregon adventure."

"Then we'll just have to make sure it's memorable." He had a mischievous smirk on his face as he slid into the car beside her. "I've got a picnic lunch and a full tank of gas. Which direction do you want to go? North, south or east — can't go west."

When he had left her at the door to her condo last night, Renzo had promised to spend the day with her today. Now the choice was up to her. Decisions, decisions...

"Let's head south," she decided, "and stop at every beach we see."

"We won't get but about 20 miles from here if we do that." he said, frowning slightly, "but your wish is my command."

She wouldn't have thought it possible, but today was even better than yesterday. They drove south on the coast highway, stopping frequently to watch the waves crash onto the shore. Several times they parked the car and walked along the beach, playing "catch me if you can" with the surf.

Once Renzo scooped her up and threatened to drop her in a tidal pool. But their laughter turned to breathless anticipation as she clung to his neck, and he was forced to place her quickly on her feet. Needing to expunge the adrenaline surge, she challenged him to race back to the car and sped off across the sand.

At noon, they sat on a blanket in a stand of twisted, wind-beaten juniper and watched the ever changing, always the same, motion of the waves upon the sand while they ate sandwiches and fruit from the basket he had produced from the car.

"Renzo," she said quietly, "what's happening between us?"

His back stiffened as he tried to remain nonchalant. "Nothing. We're good friends enjoying the sites."

"I don't think so," she said thoughtfully, watching as he carefully avoided her eyes. "I may be young and inexperienced, but... "

"That's just it," he interrupted, almost angrily, "you're not just young, you're an infant. Do you remember how old I am?"

Gwen turned her face away and smiled. His agitation told her more than he realized. She was in no hurry. They were immortal, after all.

"I remember, Renzo," she said at last, "but you should remember that I'm not a mortal woman. I'm an *Old One*, too... and you're closer to my age than anyone else."

He opened his mouth to reply, stopped to reconsider, and closed his mouth with a snap. Gwen handed him an apple and let the subject drop.

Soon after their picnic, they drove through Depoe Bay. Seeing an advertisement for a whale watching tour, Gwen talked Renzo into joining her on a two hour charter. The experience was exhilarating, though Gwen seemed happy just to be out on the water. True to their boast of being able to find whales nearly any day of the year, the crew soon pointed out water spouts to the passengers. As their vessel drew as close as legally allowed, Gwen watched in delight as a massive tail flipped above the water and then slapped the surface as the gigantic mammal dived for the ocean depths. The beast's proximity obviously enchanted her.

Renzo, however, was totally unaware of the whale's performance. Gwen absorbed his attention. He hadn't realized he'd become jaded, but being around her was like a breath of fresh air. Everything delighted her.

Having lived for nearly 600 years, there wasn't much that surprised him anymore. At least there hadn't been until he'd approached her on the beach. His reactions to her were a source of constant surprise.

He really needed to get himself under control. She hadn't even lived a quarter of a century yet... talk about robbing the cradle. No matter, he wasn't about to act on his impulses.

He would take up where Dylan left off. He would be her self-appointed body guard. Every moment with her would be cherished, and he would make damn certain that Lilith never harmed her.

Guinevere Enid Vaughan's safety and happiness were now his personal mission, and no one had better try to get between him and his duty. He watched her radiant face in the glow of the afternoon light and smiled in self-satisfaction. He had his priorities straight. He knew who he was, and what he was about.

He was an *Old One*, and he was in control of his destiny.

CHAPTER 14

*G*wen hadn't needed her radio, CDs, or audio books for the return trip to Boulder. Her mind worked a mile a minute the entire two days.

Renzo.

Lorenzo Alan Santini.

Gwen's thoughts flitted around the subject like a hummingbird approaching nectar. Never staying long on any one point, but never leaving the subject completely.

She was undeniably infatuated with Mr. Santini.

"You've found a guy." Emily squealed with excitement when she saw the dreamy expression on Gwen's face. "Details. I want details. Come on, you can't hold out on your roommate. Especially after the boring existence you've led since Christmas."

"Well," Gwen said with a giggle, "his name is Renzo, and we met at Cannon Beach — that's on the Oregon coast — and he's really nice."

"Really nice?" Emily rolled her eyes and hit herself squarely between the eyes in mock despair. "Come on, girl. You can do better than that. How old is he? Is he handsome?

"Okay. Okay." Gwen searched her brain for safe comments to make about an immortal *Old One*. "He's really good looking, in a rugged sort of way. He has dark hair — almost black; and deep, dark brown eyes. I think his eyes are his best feature. Rich chocolate with beautiful dark, curly lashes... you know, the kind most of our girlfriends would kill for." Gwen laughed, gaiety ringing in the sound. "He's older than we are — but you know how it is, I wouldn't want to guess at his age." She paused to give Emily a wicked little smile. "But he's definitely in his prime."

"So where does he live? What does he do?" Emily pushed. There was no way she was giving up on this juicy bit of conversation.

"I'm not sure, exactly," Gwen hedged, "he mentioned California. I think he's a scientific type... " Her voice trailed off.

Emily stared at her roommate in alarm. "Tell me you got his phone number, at least."

"Oh, don't worry. We know how to contact each other." As she said this, Gwen's eyes drifted into a dreamy expression.

Emily smiled as she recognized the vacant expression on her friend's face. This dreaminess was normal for their age group. She could deal with an infatuated friend. The workaholic girl she'd been living with for the past three months or so, now that was unnerving. She'd been worried about Gwen ever since they got back from Christmas break. Emily didn't want to pry, but she felt certain that something had happened to her friend. Well, at least Gwen seemed to be snapping out of it. Whoever this Renzo was, he was good for Gwen, and Emily was delighted.

~

ONCE CLASSES GOT UNDERWAY, Gwen didn't have time to moon around about Renzo. She had just over a month before finals and the due date for her thesis. The *Old One* celebration of Beltane would be held on the night of April 30th, and she would have until evening on May 1st to recover the second sign. Her thesis was due by 5:00 pm on Friday, May 3rd, with finals taking place the following Monday, Tuesday and Wednesday. After that came commencement, which would take place on Friday, May 10th.

The next six weeks were going to be *very* busy!

Dylan relieved a little of the pressure that first week back by announcing his satisfaction with her progress in her arcane studies.

"You've accomplished the goals I had in mind," he said, offering her a chocolate chip cookie as they sat in his office on Friday afternoon. "You know how to study arcane texts; you've discovered your purpose; you've begun your quest; and you've survived a couple magical attacks without assistance from a more experienced *Old One*." He ticked her accomplishments off on his fingers, his face reflecting his pride. "My only remaining responsibility as your mentor is to oversee your initiation rite into the larger family of *Old Ones*."

Gwen looked startled. "Initiation rite? You've never mentioned that before."

"Haven't I?" Dylan's eyebrows shot up, then lowered into a slight frown. "Well, no matter. There's not much to it. Nothing for you to be concerned about. It'll happen at Beltane. You'll be introduced to the *Old One* community as a whole. Merlin will welcome you... "

"Merlin?" Gwen's tea cup rattled in its saucer and she quickly set it down to avoid spilling the contents. "Are you telling me Merlin is real?"

"Why the surprise? Didn't you find his name in the Gramarye?" Dylan watched her color rise. He made a valiant attempt to hide his amusement by taking a sip of tea.

"Well, now that you mention it, I do remember seeing his name." Glancing down at her hands, Gwen remembered what it was like to be a child and forget the answer in class. Looking up again, she caught the amusement in Dylan's eyes and defiance surfaced. "You're not going to tell me this is the same guy who lived backwards and taught King Arthur."

"As a matter of fact, Arthur was his most troublesome charge. The getting younger instead of older nonsense was just an acknowledgment of the fact that he didn't age, while Arthur did. Honestly, Gwen. You know that most of human mythology is just half-forgotten *Old One* lore."

Dylan took a bite of his cookie, stood and walked to the window. As he passed, he patted Gwen's shoulder. "Merlin functions as our Chief *Old One*. A purely honorary title as he has no true authority over any of us. He is, however, one of our eldest and most respected members."

Gwen closed her eyes and sighed; someday all of this would be old news to her, but sometimes she wondered just how long that was going to take.

"Anyway, what was I saying? Oh, yes... Merlin will welcome you, and since you're doing so well, he'll relieve me of my responsibility for your health and safety. Then he'll ask the community in general to signify their acceptance of you by reciting the blessing. Finally, he'll ask for two volunteers, a female and a male, to act as your sponsors until the next Beltane fellowship."

"Nice. What do sponsors do?" Eyes wide open again, Gwen watched Dylan eagerly as he returned to his seat.

"They take up where I leave off. Check up on you from time to time. Make themselves available to answer questions — by mind-speech or in person. Just help you out, give you encouragement, that sort of thing. I'm usually the male sponsor. I'm so accustomed to watching over young *Old Ones*, I usually just continue the process. At any rate, whether I'm your official sponsor or not, I'll always be available to you — but I won't be following you to Portland."

Gwen found this last comment very reassuring. She had come to rely on Dylan, and didn't like the idea of finding herself completely cut off from him. "Thanks, Dylan. You're right, it doesn't sound like anything to worry about. My main concern about Beltane is that I haven't found a new clue yet. I don't know where to look for the second sign." She picked up her backpack and stood to leave. "I'm not going to worry about it, though. High Magic wants me to find the blasted thing, so I'm sure it'll give me a clue in time."

Dylan smiled and walked her to the door of the building. "You're right, of course. You'll find what you need at exactly the right moment."

CHAPTER 15

*A*pril 30th found Gwen in the mood to celebrate. Her printer was industriously spitting out pages of her completed thesis, a full three days before the deadline. She could probably turn it in today, but why rush? Tomorrow would be soon enough.

Besides, now that the paper was finished, and she knew she had the time, why not add an extra flourish and have the manuscript bound? That would be the perfect final touch. She'd take it to a printing shop tomorrow and wait while they did the work.

Running her hands through her hair, she thought about the coming night. Beltane would officially begin at sundown, and Dylan would escort her to the *Old One* celebration. Once there, Gwen would be initiated into the community of her peers.

She could hardly wait to see Renzo again. Well over a month had passed since they'd parted at Cannon Beach, and Gwen didn't like to admit, even to herself, how much the thought of seeing him excited her.

At least she wouldn't have to worry about what to wear.

This was one of the few times that *Old Ones* donned formal robes. Everyone in attendance would be dressed in the same fluid silver robes Dylan had worn when he introduced her to the Gramarye. Gwen's successful studies of arcane lore had earned her the right to wear those silver robes. However, because she was an initiate, tonight her robe would be belted with a scarlet rope and she would be barefoot.

Dylan had been a little vague about where the ceremony would take place, but it really didn't matter. Wherever they were, she would be comfortably warm, even without shoes.

Magic definitely had its benefits when it came to creature comforts.

Emily came in looking a bit stressed and threw herself on the couch. "I'll be so glad when the next two weeks are over." she whined. "I'm just not built to handle stress."

Gwen worked to keep a straight face. She refrained from pointing out that if Emily had kept up with her work all semester, she wouldn't need to cram now. Instead, Gwen put on a bright smile and made an effort to encourage her frazzled roommate.

"You're doing great, Em. Just keep up the good work. You'll make it to commencement yet. What are you up to tonight?"

Emily sighed and rolled her eyes. "Studying, of course. I've got to crank out a ten page paper before noon tomorrow." She seemed genuinely surprised when she saw Gwen reach for a jacket. "Where are you going?"

"I'm taking a break tonight. I finished my thesis, and I'm celebrating with a party. Don't wait up. I may crash with one of the other girls."

"A party?" Emily groaned. "I'm *so* jealous." She stood, crossed the room and gave Gwen a quick hug. "Actually, I'm very proud. You're finally getting out in the world again. And congrats on the thesis. I'm sure glad I didn't have to do one. Have a blast."

CHAPTER 16

*G*wen and Dylan stood in his office in the linguistics department with the door closed and warded. In preparation for the ceremony, they changed their mundane clothes into the silver robes of the *Old Ones*.

"So, where exactly are we going?" Gwen asked for at least the tenth time.

"You'll see when we get there," Dylan said, as he had every other time she'd asked. Far from appearing silly in his robe, her mentor looked masterful, almost austere. His stern appearance kept Gwen from questioning him too closely.

Dylan circled Gwen, checking every detail of her garb. He'd been meticulous about tying the scarlet rope, measuring the size of the knot as well as the length of the trailing ends. He'd insisted her hair be loose. No ornamentation, not even a clip for control. Now he stared at her feet.

"Sorry, Gwen," he said as he traced a small sigil, "but that nail polish has to go."

"Hands too?" she asked, extending her cherry-tipped fingers for his inspection.

"Definitely," he replied with a wry grin. "Thanks for reminding me."

When her appearance met his specifications, Dylan held out his left hand. "Take my hand, Lady. I will escort you to the ceremony." With her right hand firmly in his left, he sketched the teleportation sigil in the air, and they disappeared from his office.

When Gwen's eyes came into focus again, they stood outdoors, on cool grass, in a soft misty atmosphere. It was nearing midnight at this location, for the silver orb of the moon was nearly overhead. Gwen noted these details with little conscious thought. She was too overawed by the looming presence, the absolute majesty of the massive standing stones.

When she managed to speak, her voice was little more than a whisper. "Stonehenge... this has to be Stonehenge."

Dylan gave her hand a squeeze, then let it fall to her side. "It is, and it isn't," he said cryptically. "This is Stonehenge, but because of the prevalent magic of this special night, we're able to conduct our gathering out of phase with the mortal world. If you are completely still and concentrate your mind very precisely, you will be able to see the silhouette of the mortals who are conducting their own ceremony at this same time."

Gwen shivered and looked around more closely. She only saw her fellow *Old One*s, arriving singly or in small groups.

"We choose to ignore the mortals," Dylan continued, "their rites have no bearing on our own celebration."

Gwen nodded and followed as Dylan led her past groups of silver robed *Old One*s, chatting in low voices, to the center of the standing stones. When they reached the bearded *Old One* standing by the altar stone, Dylan bowed from the waist.

"Lord Merlin, may I present our initiate, the Lady Guinevere?"

Gwen found herself staring into a set of penetrating, tawny brown eyes. She was reminded forcefully of the uncompromising stare of a powerful bird of prey. Then a smile lit his face and the twinkle in those eyes disguised their latent authority.

"Guinevere." Her name was a benediction as it fell from his lips. "I am pleased to meet you at last. Be welcome among us."

Turning to Dylan, Merlin laid a hand on his shoulder. "You have prepared her well, Dylan. Be at ease, your task is complete." Dylan bowed again, and melted into the throng which crowded the turf between the ring of sarsen stones and the array of trilithons which formed a horseshoe around the altar stone.

Merlin picked up his staff, which had been lying against the Altar Stone, and held it aloft. The crystal at its tip began to glow with a pure silver sheen and a clear, sweet pattern of musical notes caressed Gwen's ears. The crowd quieted to hear the melody, and all eyes were drawn to the light.

Bringing the staff to rest at his side, Merlin began. "We come together twice each year, at Samhain and Beltane, to celebrate as a family." He paused, allowing his gaze to sweep his audience. "This year is special indeed, for we welcome a new *Old One* to our circle. The Lady Guinevere is awake." He held out his hand to Gwen and drew her into the center of the assembled *Old Ones'* attention.

Gwen suddenly felt very young and awkward, aware that the beings scrutinizing her were many thousands of years old. Her cheeks burned and panic threatened to overwhelm her, when she found an anchor to hold her steady.

Lorenzo.

Relief washed over her as their eyes locked. His gaze affirmed her worth.

Calm again, she returned her attention to Merlin's words.

"Lord Dylan has done an admirable job on her training. The Lady Guinevere has both discovered and begun her first quest." There was a soft exclamation of surprise from the assembled *Old Ones*. "Indeed," Merlin continued, "we have all been amazed by the rapidity of her progress."

Merlin turned to face Gwen, his hawk-bright eyes peering deep into her own. "Lady Guinevere, do you accept the authority of High Magic in your life, and will you swear to serve it faithfully, maintaining the balance of Light and Dark to the best of your ability?"

Gwen met his gaze and answered in a clear, strong voice, "I do and I will."

The gathered *Old Ones* cheered and applauded.

Merlin faced the crowd, waiting for them to quiet. When he judged the moment ripe, he called for their attention.

"It has been many long centuries since I have asked this assembly for volunteers to sponsor a young *Old One*. But I ask now: which lady among you will guide Guinevere as she matures in our ways?"

Gwen glanced shyly at the crowd, and was pleased to see Mei make her way to the Altar Stone. "I will gladly provide the Lady Guinevere with the benefit of my experience." Smiling reassuringly, she traced a sigil in the air and produced a pair of leather sandals. Stooping, she helped Gwen step into the intricately decorated footwear.

Merlin nodded at Mei, and turned again to the assembly. "Now, a Lord is required to stand beside Guinevere, to guide her decisions if she asks, and to defend her life should she have that need. Who will come forward?"

As Merlin spoke, Gwen sought Dylan in the crowd. He'd said he would accept this role, but before he could move or even speak, another *Old One* made his way to Merlin's side.

"I will guard the Lady's safety," Lorenzo said, "and her happiness as well, if it is within my power." Ignoring the murmurings of the crowd — they had clearly expected Dylan to assume that role — Lorenzo produced a sigil-laden belt of finely wrought silver fashioned in a pattern of interconnecting leaves. Mei removed the scarlet rope from Gwen's waist, and Renzo fastened the belt in place.

When he smiled and gazed into her eyes, Gwen thought she might explode with happiness.

Right there, in front of Merlin and everyone.

Merlin cleared his throat, pulling Gwen and Renzo back to the *Old One* gathering. "Now that you are fully garbed and shod, it is my honor to give you the final implement of your *Old One* power."

He traced a sigil and presented Gwen with a magnificent staff. With its base firmly planted in the dirt at her feet, its carved crystal top stood just higher than her head. Made of polished oak, the crystal's setting was a dazzling knotwork of gleaming gold.

Stunned by its beauty, Gwen accepted the staff. The moment her hand touched the smooth surface of the wood, she knew she'd found a missing part of herself. A part she hadn't known existed, hadn't expected, but a necessary piece to her completion as a magical being.

She gazed at Merlin through a sheen of tears, and wondered if she would be in trouble if she threw her arms around his neck and hugged him until someone dragged her off?

His smiling expression told her that he understood the depth of her reaction.

"Dear family," Merlin cried, "let us welcome our new sister into our ranks with a blessing." The entire assembly, including Mei and Renzo, who stood on each side of her, recited the litany.

> May the blessing of Light be upon you,
> Light without, and Light within.
>
> May the harmony of Balance be with you,
> Balance without, and Balance within.
>
> May the gift of intuition be upon you,
> May the blessing of High Magic be yours.

When the blessing was finished, Merlin's hold on the group deteriorated and Gwen was rushed by *Old Ones* wanting to meet her, hug her, welcome her into her new family.

The experience was heady.

Quite some time passed before she became aware of Merlin's attempt to call the throng back to order. Taking her place in the crowd, Gwen found herself sandwiched between Mei and Renzo, with Dylan standing directly behind her. Unable to resist the impulse, she turned and gave him a quick hug, then obediently gave Merlin her attention.

"On a serious note, we are deeply saddened by the death of our estranged brother, Samuel. Though he strayed from the path of Light, while he lived we could hope he would awaken from the

Dark's enthrallment." He stopped and gazed around the circle of his friends and family. "We cannot truly mourn his death, for it means his power is no longer available to Lilith for the Dark's vile purposes, but we do mourn the loss of the potential his life once held." He paused, and produced a small candle.

"To Samuel," he cried, holding the candle aloft. "His light was shielded by the Dark," his hand formed a screen around the candle, "but now it has been extinguished." He pinched the wick between his fingers; the tiny flame went out. "A light is lost, a light is gained. Let us celebrate the Light."

With that, the Beltane festival truly began. Gwen was delighted with the variety of activities that the night held. Sensory overload was a definite concern at this event.

The traditional lighting of the Beltane fire, signifying the return of light and life after winter's icy grip, was an unanticipated treat. Bonfires had always been favorite events for Gwen.

The May Pole was amazing. Decorated from top to bottom with carved sigils, it was a sight to behold, even before intricate designs were created by weaving red and white streamers around it.

Then there were the dances. Circle dances were performed on the grounds outside the sarsen stones, while line dancers wove complicated patterns around and between the ancient standing stones.

Gwen wandered among her people and absorbed the assault on her senses. The music was indescribable. Bards sang the history of her people, while small ensembles played lively jigs and reels. She heard everything from gentle notes being coaxed from an Irish harp to the raucous, joyful shout of bagpipes.

The scents wafting on the air around her were an olfactory feast. Tables laden with delicacies appeared along the Avenue — the entrance lane that ran northeast from the sarsen circle — and spices from around the world vied to capture the merrymakers' attention. It was like a fabulous cross between a county fair and a large family reunion, and Gwen was determined to enjoy every single bit of it.

Finally, just before dawn lit the sky, Merlin called his people together again and introduced Sibyl, the *Old One*'s chief prophet.

"For the sake of our youngest sister, I will remind you that we end every gathering of our clan with the recitation of our most sacred prophecy." She closed her eyes for a moment, then opened them and exclaimed, "Hear me now, *Old Ones*.

> A promise was made, it will come to pass.
> High Magic has spoken, this shall be at last.
> A man and a maid of Old Ones fair,
> Shall give to the world its Chosen heir.
>
> The Heir shall be mighty, the Heir shall be great.
> True balance establish… the Chosen One's fate.
> While the Chosen holds balance, mankind will
>   mature,
> And spring from the earth, to the stars' bright
>   allure.

When she finished, she lowered her head, murmured, "Let it be soon." and disappeared into the crowd.

Merlin took her place, raised his staff, and said in a mighty voice, "Blessings upon you. We shall meet again at Samhain." Then he struck his staff on the Altar Stone, and vanished.

"Merlin has always enjoyed making a theatrical exit." Renzo's breath tickled her ear as he spoke. Gwen smiled and turned to find Mei and Dylan standing there as well.

"Before we leave," said Mei, "do you have any questions you'd like us to help you clear up?"

Now that the excitement of the festival was ebbing away, Gwen realized she still had a task to accomplish before sundown. "Well, the most pressing matter is that I haven't a clue where I'm supposed to look for my second quest sign. I don't suppose any of you know anything?" Gwen didn't really expect a response, but a girl could always hope. As they shook their heads, she sighed. "I didn't really think you would. But, I do have a question," her face brightened with the new thought, "what was all that nonsense about the prophecy Sibyl recited?"

All three of them stared at her, shock registering on their faces.

"Nonsense?" Mei asked incredulously.

Gwen, surprised by their reactions, hurried to explain her comment. "Well, I mean, I thought prophecy was supposed to help you pinpoint stuff. What kind of a clue is it that an *Old One* couple is going to have a son? I mean really. Which couple? Which son? How is that specific?"

Suddenly, Dylan and Renzo both seemed to be completely absorbed in studying the weave of the fabric of their robes. Neither of them would meet her eyes. Since the men didn't appear inclined to speak, Gwen gave up and looked to Mei for enlightenment.

Mei didn't seem too eager to meet her eyes either, but finally gave in with a sigh. "It is a very specific prophecy, Gwen. I'm sorry, I hadn't realized you didn't fully understand our nature." Taking Gwen's hand, she met her gaze directly and said, "No *Old*

One woman has ever given birth, Gwen. We do not bear children."

Gwen stared at her, struggling to understand the simple words.

"It's not just the women, either," said Dylan with equal delicacy, "no *Old One* man has ever fathered a child, whether his partner was *Old One* or human. We do not have children. *You* are our most recent child."

Suddenly the pieces fell into place and Gwen saw the whole picture. There had been no children here tonight, neither had there been any pregnant women. These people lived forever, but they had no intimate family relationships. Once their birth families died, they were alone... except for their clan-like connection to one another.

These people... her people... she, Guinevere Enid Vaughan, would never have a child.

Before the enormity of this realization could fully penetrate her psyche, Gwen was called back to reality by a young woman touching her arm and calling her name.

"I'm sorry," she said, turning to face the speaker, "were you talking to me?"

"I was," said the young woman. She had sleek black hair and almond eyes which spoke eloquently of her Asian heritage. Indian, Gwen guessed, thinking she would be stunning in a sari.

"My name is Veesa Aramugham, Lady Guinevere, and I believe I have a message for you." She smiled and bowed gracefully before continuing. "I came across this short prophecy in my studies in Calcutta. High Magic suggested that I would find the *Old One* it was intended for here, at our Beltane festival."

Gwen's mouth fell open. "High Magic suggested?" She actually squeaked, her surprise was so great. "You can *talk* to High Magic?"

Veesa's voice rippled with laughter. "Not in normal conversation, no, but interpretation is my gift. I sense the deeper meaning behind what is said or written. I knew this prophecy was not meant for me, and it was obvious its intended reader would be revealed at this gathering. You are the *Old One* I seek." She handed a small square of parchment to Gwen, who unfolded it and read it immediately.

"Oh." she cried, "thank you, Veesa. And thanks be to High Magic as well." She glanced around excitedly at her companions. "Dylan, Renzo, it's the clue for the sign I must find today."

"Wonderful." Dylan congratulated her heartily, relieved that Gwen's attention had been drawn away from the topic of *Old One* fecundity. "What does it say?"

Glancing at the parchment again, Gwen read:

> As the Dark of the Year dies and Light is reborn,
> Old Ones gather, a maypole to adorn.
> On this Arcane High Day, all celebrate,
> For summer is coming, warmth and plenty await.
>
> Seek me where the mountains rise to the sky,
> On the roof of the world you will find me, just try.
> I am breath, I am breeze, I am a whiff of heaven
> Seek me where I waft, the second sign of seven."

Gwen smiled at the small group of *Old Ones* surrounding her. "I don't know what it means, but I'm sure glad to finally have it in my hand."

"Perhaps I can help," Veesa offered. "You may not be aware of this, but in my country Mt. Everest is often referred to as *the roof of the world*."

"Yes," said Dylan excitedly, "and while your first sign was a manifestation of fire, it sounds like this one will be an example of wind; another of the four elemental spirits."

"Thank you so much, Veesa." Gwen gave the other woman an enthusiastic hug. "Thanks for bringing me the clue, and for helping me understand it. Looks like I'm off to Mt. Everest." Gwen's eyes shone as she contemplated this new adventure.

"You are most welcome, little sister. Blessings upon you." Veesa bowed with a smile and disappeared.

Gwen gazed expectantly at Dylan. "So, shall we seek from here, or return to your office?"

Sighing, Dylan reached for Gwen's hand before answering. "I have been relieved, Lady. There are others who will aid you in your quest now." Seeing the rebellion brewing on her face, he added hurriedly, "I will always be available to advise you, Gwen, but it would be inappropriate for me to stand between you and those who have pledged to support you." He smiled and kissed her hand. "Blessings upon you, Lady. I leave you with capable mentors." Then he, too, disappeared.

CHAPTER 17

Standing in front of the massive Altar Stone, surrounded by imposing trilithons, and beyond them, the mighty sarsen stones, Gwen felt very small and insignificant. She also felt strangely vulnerable without Dylan's reassuring presence.

Mei placed a hand lightly on Gwen's shoulder, bringing her back to the moment. "I am happy to stand watch while you search." Her voice was calm and soothing. "However, I have great faith in your ability, so I am also happy to leave you to your work, if that is your desire." Mei glanced at Renzo, and he nodded his agreement.

Gwen felt slightly sick at the thought of being left alone here in this awe-inspiring place. She closed her eyes, took a deep breath and battled the wave of panic until her emotions were firmly under her control. Opening her eyes, she smiled wryly at her sponsors. "It may be a weakness," she said, "but I'm new enough to this whole process that I'd really appreciate it if you watched over me."

Mei simply nodded, but Renzo cleared his throat to speak. "It's not weakness, Gwen. We all needed support as we learned our way through this maze of power."

"Indeed," added Mei, "sponsors would be unnecessary if you were expected to do everything on your own. I simply meant that it is your choice, and if you prefer solitude to work, then you shall have it."

"Thank you, both of you." Gwen's face brightened. She was grateful for her new friends' understanding. "Dylan linked with my mind at Alban Eiler and followed me to the sign." She glanced hopefully at Renzo. "Can you watch where I go, and come if I need you?" He looked a little disappointed, so she hurried to explain in more detail. "I mean, I'd like to try to retrieve the sign on my own this time. But I'll feel much safer if I know you'll come if anything goes wrong."

Renzo glanced from Gwen to Mei, then back again. "Yes, I can do that. I'll link with your mind and follow your search. Mei, will you monitor Mt. Everest? We're fairly sure that's where she'll be going, so if you monitor the peak, you'll be able to alert us to any traps."

Mei nodded. "A sensible division of responsibility." Immediately, she lapsed into a far-seeing trance.

"All right then," said Gwen in as brisk a tone as she could manage, "it's time I got to work."

Renzo agreed, sketching a sigil in the air between them. Instantly she was aware that a quiet corner of her mind was now occupied, and that the occupation felt completely natural. Renzo's mind-touch emanated warmth and comfort.

Closing her eyes, Gwen entered the gelatinous bubble once again — a place where she was rapidly coming to feel secure and at ease. The bubble was part of her power, something she was learning to acknowledge as a legitimate part of her being. Sending her consciousness in search was not a source of agitation this time. It was more of a release of tension; she was doing what she'd been born to do and it was very liberating.

Gwen imagined that this wild joy was akin to what an eagle felt as he rode the wind currents high into the sky. Reluctantly, she reined her elation in, and forced herself to concentrate on the sign she sought. Wrenching her vision away from the limitless expanse of space, Gwen gazed to the southeast, towards Asia and Mt. Everest. Layer by layer the distance fell away between where she stood and that lofty pinnacle.

There.

The soft golden glow she had come to associate with the object of a search pulsed in the distance. Gwen concentrated on that glow, forcing the intervening space to peel away, leaving a trail in her mind that would guide her inexorably — if she chose to approach her target in a mundane fashion.

Gwen reveled in the knowledge that her power gave her such a variety of options. She knew that time was short for the accomplishment of this task, so she would teleport when the exact location became clear, but it was fascinating to realize that a physical map was being imprinted on her brain as she sought.

She still had moments of pure amazement, to know that magic was real and she was a magician, a wizard, a wielder of supernatural knowledge. She still felt the need to pinch herself; this was all so unreal...

In an instant, her arcane search ended. Clearly defined in her mind's eye, Gwen saw the exact spot she would need to stand in order to reach out and touch the glowing golden orb. With a cry of delight, she teleported.

This time the compression that accompanied her physical flight held no terror. She knew that she could bear the pressure, and waited expectantly for the relief of expansion. When she materialized at the summit of the roof of the world, Gwen threw her arms out, and laughingly spun around in giddy delight. She was an *Old One*. She had a task to do, and she was good at it!

As the giddiness faded, Gwen recalled where she was and knew she must hurry. Even an *Old One* could only withstand the grueling conditions of this altitude for a limited time. She oriented herself on the golden glow. Under the compulsion of her presence, it was rapidly solidifying into the second sign — the sign of wind.

The sign hung in the air, a few feet above the ground, right at the highest point of the great mountain's peak: a dew-drenched spider web, glistening in the reddening light of the setting sun. As she stepped forward to claim the sign, the air wavered in front of her...

...and Lilith appeared.

Immediately she was aware of agitation from the being occupying the warm corner of her mind. *No*, she commanded Renzo, *I can do this. Trust me.* She felt his uneasiness, but knew he would make no effort to materialize.

"You can't harm me, Lilith." Gwen stood straight and proud, assured of her authority in this situation. "Why bother with this charade?"

"I don't have to harm you, child, or even use magic against you. I only have to prevent you from taking hold of that sign before the sun sets." Lilith's eyes glowed with malignant satisfaction. "You should not have waited so long, little sister."

Gwen studied her adversary for a moment, seeking her weakness. "You can't use magic against me, Lilith, even to defend yourself." She paused, giving Lilith time to catch the implied threat in her statement. "High Magic desires that I win that sign, therefore I am free to use magic against you to attain it. Do you really wish to face my power when you're unable to defend yourself?" She watched comprehension dawn on Lilith's lovely face.

"You wouldn't use magic against me when I can't fight back." The snarl in the older woman's voice was unmistakable. "It's not who you are. I wouldn't hesitate, but you're not that cold-blooded."

"Don't underestimate my resolve. Are you willing to bet your life on my goodness?" Gwen gave her a dazzling smile that didn't quite reach her eyes. "As you pointed out, my time is limited. Your window of opportunity to leave unscathed is rapidly closing." She glanced past Lilith to the sign, shimmering in the sun's glow. Gwen lifted her hand to draw a sigil, paused and looked squarely into Lilith's eyes. "Decision time. Depart... or accept the consequences."

Lilith's expression was both angry and frustrated, but she disappeared without another word.

Once her adversary was gone, Gwen wasted no time. She grabbed the sign immediately. Before she could even think about drawing the sigil to return to Stonehenge, Renzo appeared in front of her.

A storm raged in his eyes as he scowled down at her from his full height. Gwen knew he was taller than she, but his anger seemed to add inches. "What do you think you were doing?" The words rang out in the rarified air. "She's very dangerous, and you're very inexperienced. I can't believe you ordered me to stay put."

He paced around her, scowling. "Worse, I can't believe I was constrained to obey. What was High Magic doing? What were you thinking?"

Gwen stood quietly, waiting for his rant to die out. She was more than a little irritated by his assumption that she was helpless and inexperienced. She'd done just fine, thank you very much. He should be praising her for her ingenuity. On the other hand, she was pleased that he cared enough to be ranting and raving about her supposed close call with disaster. She knew Dylan would have been concerned about her, but she couldn't imagine Dylan throwing the tantrum Renzo was subjecting her to.

When he finally wound down, Gwen calmly held up the sign and brought it into contact with her bracelet. They watched as it diminished and attached itself to the link next to the black lava sign. It sparkled on her wrist, a tiny spider web of light.

"Thank you for your assistance, Renzo," she said quietly, "and thank you for trusting me to complete my own task." Suddenly, she threw her arms around his neck. "I did it. I found the second sign, and even Lilith couldn't stop me!"

Her enthusiasm was contagious. Renzo laughed out loud as he hugged her tightly, lifting her off her feet. "You certainly did. You scared me to death in the process, but you certainly did. All on your own, you did it." Giving her a final squeeze, he placed her back on her own two feet. "We should get back to Mei. She'll want to congratulate you as well."

Grinning like fools, they teleported back to the Altar Stone.

CHAPTER 18

*D*ylan looked at her in amazement as Gwen described her encounter with Lilith on the summit of Mt. Everest.

"...and then she just left, and I ran to get the sign. I couldn't believe it." Remembered triumph glowed on her flushed face.

"That's quite an achievement. Facing down the Dark Queen... and you say Renzo was aware of all this?" Dylan broke into a hearty grin. "I'll bet he was fit to be tied."

"Well, yes," she admitted, "he did bellow quite a bit after it was all over."

"Bellow?" Dylan roared with laughter. "I'll just bet he did. Actually, keeping him from materializing to rescue you is almost as impressive as besting Lilith."

Gwen frowned in puzzlement. "He said something like that when he was yelling at me. Like I prevented him from coming. At the time, I thought he was just honoring my request. But you both sound like I placed some kind of compulsion on him."

Dylan sobered at once. "You mean you didn't use a compulsion sigil when you gave the command?"

"Heavens no." exclaimed Gwen, "I wouldn't dream of compelling Renzo to do, or even not do, anything."

"Well, well." Dylan stroked his chin as he considered her words. "High Magic seems to be taking your wishes very seriously — at least as far as this quest is concerned. How interesting, I'll have to give this matter some serious thought. Did Mei make any comments?"

"Only to apologize for not being able to forewarn me of Lilith's presence," she replied, "but I told her that was silly, how could she know what Lilith was going to do before she did it? Her only responsibility was to let me know that she wasn't there with a bunch of her thugs before I arrived." Gwen paused to have a sip of cola. "Mei did say she was very proud of the way I handled myself. She didn't say she was surprised, but her eyes and voice certainly implied it."

"Don't let that bother you," Dylan said firmly, "I know you much better than Mei does, and I'm absolutely flabbergasted at what you did. What would you have done if Lilith had called your bluff?"

"What makes you think it was a bluff, Dylan?" The coldness in her voice startled him. "I would have blasted her without a second thought." When he continued to stare, Gwen shrugged. "If you recall our discussion at Christmas, you and Renzo made it pretty clear to me she was responsible for my parents' death. I won't actively seek to harm her, but if she gets in my way, I won't hesitate to kill her."

Dylan nodded mutely and tactfully changed the subject. "So, tell me your plans for this merry month of May."

Gwen smiled at his choice of words. "Since I finished my thesis before Beltane, I have the rest of the week off. I'll probably spend most of it in the library reviewing for finals." She took another sip of her rapidly flattening cola, made a face, then sketched a sigil to refresh it. "I'm really lucky, my exams are all on Monday and Tuesday. That gives me all day Wednesday and Thursday to pack. Commencement is Friday morning, and Aunt Katie and Uncle Jem are coming down from the ranch for that. I'll follow them home on Friday afternoon. What I can't fit in my Jeep, Uncle Jem will manage to pack into his."

"That sounds like a very efficient plan," agreed Dylan. "When do you leave for Portland?"

"I got a letter from Mrs. Gresham the other day, confirming that I can take possession of the apartment on June 3rd. I'm planning to leave on June 1st to allow myself two full days to get there. At least this time I know exactly where I'm going."

"Will you stay at the ranch between commencement and your big move?"

"I think so. This has been a very... shall we say unusual?... semester. I don't feel the need to take a vacation or have an adventure. Being around the familiar ranch routine for a couple of weeks sounds like heaven right now."

"When will Katie and Jem get to see your new place?"

"There's been some discussion about them helping me move, but I haven't encouraged it. I mean, I'd be delighted to have the help, and I'd love for them to see where I'm going to be, but it's a really busy time on the ranch, and I'd hate for them to lose income over it. I'm trying to get them to wait and come at Thanksgiving."

"That's a good choice," he agreed. "Halfway between Samhain and Alban Arthuan. Shouldn't be any *Old One* interference with their visit."

Gwen flashed him a quick grin, "My thoughts exactly. I want to keep them safely isolated from my arcane activities." Her easy smile changed to a serious expression. "By the way, Dylan, may I ask you a question, or would you prefer that I mindspeak Mei or Renzo?"

"You may always ask me anything, Gwen." Dylan leaned forward and touched her hand. "I wasn't rejecting you when I left at Beltane, merely affirming Renzo and Mei's right to take the lead."

"Thanks you." She closed her eyes for a moment, more relieved than she could express by his answer. When she opened them again, she asked, "Would you please explain my staff? I know it's important. I feel the rightness when it's in my hand, but how do I use it? Surely I don't draw sigils with something that size?"

"Evidently I didn't do as good a job preparing you as I thought," Dylan said, an embarrassed expression on his face. He stood and strode across the room as he continued, "I'll get you the proper text, but the short version is that your staff acts as a... uhm... a macro." He rummaged around in the chest that held his arcane texts, drawing out slim volume. "Yes, that's a good analogy. You know how a macro records keystrokes at the computer, then plays them back when you touch a designated key? Well, your staff can be programmed... for lack of a better word. You'll specify your preferred spells, and the staff will implement them for you. It sounds more complicated than it is." He handed her the book. "Here, study this text. It'll explain everything."

"This text?" Gwen started, recognizing the slim book in his hand. "Oh, Dylan. I'm so sorry. This isn't your fault at all. You gave me this one a week or so ago. It was in a pile with four or five others.

I was so swamped at the time... I must've missed this one." Her face flamed scarlet with shame. "But I definitely remember that cover."

The book in question was a brilliant emerald green, embossed with a wizard's staff highlighted in gold. It was a small book, but Gwen still couldn't believe she'd returned it without reading it.

"Well, no real harm done." Dylan shrugged as he sat down at his desk once more. "Still, I'm glad to know I'm not losing my touch. All these centuries, and I haven't let an *Old One* get past me untrained yet. My record remains unblemished." He chuckled lightly and winked.

Gwen laughed and sat down to read the manual on wielding a magic staff.

CHAPTER 19

*F*ootsteps stabbed through the icy halls like the pounding of an adrenaline-pumped heart. The lonely fortress sat huddled in the shadows of an enormous glacier, in a land where glaciers were as common as sand in the desert.

Antarctica.

Lilith and her minions had built their scabrous bubble of habitable space in a desolate land humans seldom chose to visit.

The palace itself should have been beautiful… a crystal confection stretching its arms to the sun and reflecting back the glorious light. Its lines and proportions had been designed with careful detail. Alas, like its mistress, the ice palace had been flawed in the execution.

Its towers, which should have been graceful spires pointing to the heavens, were treacherous stingers, rising bloated and rank in the dim Antarctic night. Inside, its halls and corridors were white tombs — bleak and desolate, devoid of warmth, color, or any spark of creature comfort. The crystalline walls rose to rafters of polished white bone. Sound carried with deadly clarity within these hollow halls. The simple tap-tap of dripping water became staccato gunshots — inflicting auditory wounds.

Lilith strode within that comfortless place, her footsteps resounding painfully, disconcerting every living creature within the icy walls. Lost in a towering rage, she railed at the indignity she'd been forced to endure at the hands of that infant, Guinevere Enid Vaughan.

The indignity was unthinkable!

Lilith, the Queen of Darkness, bested by a newly trained child. Why, the girl was barely awake, while Lilith had been the mistress of her power for eons.

The little idiot had no real strength, but she did have High Magic's favor.

How was Lilith going to get around that cursed sigil of High Magic's making? Why was this young *Old One* so well protected?

As Lilith paced, minuscule movements on the part of her servants impinged on her awareness. The fools huddled near the edges of the great hall, required to remain lest she want for something, but terrified by the rage that seethed from her restless motion. She focused her pent-up vexation on their unintentional interruption.

"Well?" Fury sparked from Lilith's eyes; her voice was raw with barely contained rage. "What do you worthless imbeciles want?"

"A thousand pardons, Great Lady." The head goblin groveled, shaking in abject terror, while the rest quickly prostrated themselves on the stone-cold floor. "We exist to please. How may we serve your Worship?"

Lilith sneered at their cowering forms. "I require intelligent thought. A task for which you have no capacity." She spun around and stalked to her throne. When she was seated, she addressed the goblins again. "Begone, and do not approach this room again unless you are summoned."

Distracted from her malevolent thoughts, she watched in disgust as the goblins slunk from the room. She needed servants, of course, but sometimes she wished she'd never created those infernal creatures. She didn't mind the grotesqueness of their physical bodies, and she appreciated the cruelty and lack of compassion that marked their basic nature, but she did wish they'd retained at least a trace of the native intelligence of the men she'd debased to create them.

Ah well, intelligence is an overrated quality in servants. she consoled herself, drumming her fingers lightly on the arm of her throne. *At least I needn't be concerned about rebellion. There isn't a flicker of creative thought among them.* She barked with laughter. The very idea of those pestilent toads rebelling was absurd.

A cruel light glinted in her eyes as a new idea flitted across her mind. *I could destroy the lot of them; start over with fresh material. Ooh, if I handle the torture and mutilation correctly,* she closed her eyes as a thrill caressed her body, *I could gain immense power from their souls' anguish before allowing them to die. Of course, then I'd need new servants.* She tapped a long forefinger to her lovely lips as she considered the possibilities.

She smiled. Long ages had passed since she'd created the goblins, but Lilith still remembered the intense physical pleasure she'd enjoyed while seducing a small army of men to her fortress. One by one, they had fallen prey to her charms.

The cretins.

Each had thought himself the sole recipient of her favors. As if any mortal could do more than satisfy a momentary itch.

Still, it had been pleasant, having all those men begging to be allowed to dip into her well of delights. She'd played with them for months, had been aroused by the depths of depravity to which she'd been able to drive them. Not a one had stood up to her.

But then, who could deny a goddess?

Each in turn had performed a succession of vile acts for her amusement, until their souls had been so tainted they no longer recognized themselves as men.

Of course, that was only the appetizer.

Next came the ultimate ecstasy — the beastialization of those insipid men. The physical intercourse was over. She no longer allowed them access to her body, but the sexual thrill of using her magic to deform their minds and souls was almost overpowering. She mangled their souls with her spells until rape, torture, and corruption were their only thoughts.

Those... and fear of Lilith.

Warped and debauched they might be, but they retained knowledge of the searing pain she could inflict. Lilith was their goddess, but terror was the only emotion she inspired.

Unfortunately, their physical bodies followed the twisted shape of their souls. Lilith ended up with an army of hideous monsters.

Still, she thought, *it might be exciting to try again, and my Old One lieutenants could use the power boost in dealing with Miss High and Mighty and her misbegotten sigil.* Lilith licked her lips, shivering with anticipation. *Perhaps I will go hunting for fresh meat soon.*

CHAPTER 20

Gwen glanced around the quadrangle at her cap-and-gown-clad peers. They'd gathered for a complimentary breakfast of coffee and pastries on the quad at 7:00 A.M., and now everyone was making final adjustments to their academic regalia before the procession to Folsom Field for the actual ceremony.

Despite Colorado's reputation for unpredictable weather, the day was perfect. Clear blue skies dotted with the occasional puffy white cloud. Grass so green it sparkled like the proverbial emerald, and air sweet with the fragrance of blossoming trees and early spring flowers.

They'd done it. Graduation Day had arrived.

Just for a moment, she was a purely human girl exulting in an accomplishment earned by four years of hard work. She had done this without magic. This moment was her own, a tribute to the human parents who could not be here, as well as to the foster family whose love had continued their legacy.

Her eyes lingered fondly on Emily as she straightened the mortarboard on Chad's head. A few feet away, Kendra and Danny clasped hands nervously as they watched the queue form.

Dana, Cassie, Angela, Dave, Brian, Ashley, Julie, Brent, Stan...

Gwen ticked off the names that went with the faces of her classmates. Friends, rivals, acquaintances. These young lives had peopled her world for the past four years, and now they were about to set out on separate paths.

For some, the parting would be final; their paths would never cross again in this mortal realm. For others, their lives would remain intertwined, the strands crossing and re-crossing, forming patterns as complex as any Celtic knot. Then there were the few committed couples, who would face the future with the unique strength that came from their harmonious union. They represented not just double strands, but sturdy ropes that would become stronger with time — as long as they honored and cherished the love that bound them.

Gwen sighed as she took her place in the line of graduates. Like the rest of them, she was filled with a curious blend of excitement, anticipation, and fear. However, her emotional mix held the added ingredient of responsibility.

She was not just a human girl about to embark on the next phase of her life. She was an *Old One*, responsible for maintaining the precarious balance between Light and Dark. A responsibility which would affect the very fabric of these mortals' lives. She was in no way responsible for their individual choices, of course, but it was her duty to give them a stable world in which to make those decisions.

A daunting prospect, indeed. Thank High Magic she wasn't alone in shouldering it.

As she listened to the speeches, her mind drifted to her circle of friends' farewell dinner. Nearly all of them had family in town for the big event, but they'd still managed to get together last night. Knowing that today would be busy and that many of them would be leaving soon after the ceremony, they had left their out-of-town guests to their own devices and gotten together for pizza.

The evening had been an emotional roller coaster — full of laughter and fun, as well as tearful good-byes. Nevertheless, Gwen was glad the fourteen of them had taken those few hours for themselves.

When the speeches ended, the graduates filed across the stage. Gwen's turn came at last. She mounted the stage, shook hands with the Dean of her college, and received her diploma case from the President of the university. The case was empty, of course. The all-important diploma would be mailed to her in a week or two, along with her final transcript. Still, as she smiled for the obligatory camera shot with the President, she glowed with pride of accomplishment.

It's official, Gwen exulted. *I've got a Bachelor of Arts degree and I'm about to start work on my Ph.D. I wonder if I'll actually finish that goal, or if High Magic's plans will interfere?*

She considered her prospects for only a moment before the rush of congratulatory hugs from friends and family drove all thoughts of High Magic and *Old Ones* from her mind.

CHAPTER 21

*G*wen stood on the threshold of her Portland apartment surveying the results of her attempt to unload the Jeep and rental trailer. After more repetitions than she cared to count, the trek from the subterranean parking garage to her third floor apartment was getting very old. The only bright spot in the path she was wearing from Jeep to living room was the existence of the elevator. Thank heavens for the wonders of mechanical engineering.

"What a mess," she sighed, glaring around her new living room with dismay. The floor was so littered with boxes it was hard to ascertain the color of the carpet. "All this effort and I've only managed to unload the Jeep."

She dropped to the floor, berating the injustice of the work-accomplished to effort-expended ratio, and shuddered at the thought of opening the tightly crammed U-Haul trailer. Uncle Jem and two of his best men had packed it for her at the ranch. Having watched them do it, Gwen knew that not so much as a centimeter of shift had occurred in transit. Those guys really knew how to fit furniture and boxes together with pinpoint precision. She appreciated the artistry of their work, but quailed at the thought of trying to break down the mountain of cargo on her own.

How had she managed to overlook the fact that she would be on her own at this end of the journey?

Aunt Katie had insisted Gwen take her bedroom furniture as well as the small recliner she loved snuggling into with a good book. She knew Katie was right. She was going to have to furnish this apartment with something... she'd just as well start with a few familiar pieces. But now those possessions lurked in the parking garage like demons ready to suck the life energy from her fragile body.

"Oh give me a break." Gwen laughed aloud at the melodrama her tired muscles were inspiring. "You're a strong healthy woman, and an *Old One* to boot. It's just a trailer full of furniture and boxes."

Settling more comfortably on the rose-brown carpet, she stretched her arms and massaged her calf muscles absently. She needed help. She could accomplish the task with magic... a quick sigil and the trailer would be empty and the room set up. But that didn't feel like a real option in this unwarded apartment complex. She didn't want to give her new neighbors nightmares about the witch who'd moved in next door.

Smiling wryly at the thought of furniture dancing its way up from the garage, and the reactions of residents who might happen to see the parade, she decided against magic. She didn't know anyone in Portland, so she couldn't call on friends, but she could mindspeak Dylan and Lorenzo. But that didn't seem fair, they'd feel obligated to come, and they wouldn't be able to use magic either.

"Wait a minute," she whooped, "I'm missing the obvious."

She jumped to her feet, and, ignoring the elevator, ran down the stairs to Mrs. Gresham's apartment. Knocking on her door, Gwen fought to catch her breath while she waited for it to open.

"Why, Gwen. How nice to see you." The gray-haired little woman stared at her new tenant in surprise. "Is there something you need, dear?" Concern creased her brow as she took in Gwen's disheveled appearance.

"Actually, there is." The red in Gwen's cheeks was slowly fading to pink as her heart rate returned to normal after her pelt down the stairs. "I was wondering if I could borrow a phone book. I need to find a moving company... someplace that could send a couple of men to unload my furniture for me."

"Of course you do." exclaimed Mrs. Gresham, "and you've come to the right place. With tenants coming and going, I'm always being asked for reliable names." She rummaged through the cubby holes in an antique Queen Anne secretary. "Yes, here it is." Turning triumphantly, she handed Gwen an index card with the names of four moving companies. "Do you need to use my phone, dear?"

"Oh, thank you so much. No, I'll use my cell phone. Should I copy these down, or may I borrow the card for a few minutes?"

"No need to do either... I've several copies of that card. Do let me know if you need anything else, dear." Mrs. Gresham smiled as she escorted Gwen back to the hall.

Several hours later, Gwen gazed around her apartment in satisfaction. There were still boxes everywhere, but real progress had been made.

She'd been lucky. The second company she'd called had a team in her area that was just finishing their morning job. They hadn't been scheduled to work an afternoon gig, but when Gwen described the size of her trailer, the dispatcher had laughed and said it would take her guys about an hour to empty a little thing like that.

So it was that shortly after the lunch hour, Gwen opened her front door to two brawny young men with work gloves and determined faces. She spent the next hour directing traffic... that box goes in that room... the bed goes in this bedroom, etcetera. The guys were even nice enough to set the bed up for her, so she wouldn't have to wrestle the heavy box springs and mattress on her own.

Gwen thanked them heartily as she made out their check, and asked them to express her sincere appreciation to the dispatcher as well. She was so relieved to have the unloading done, to not need to wait another day or two to find an available team.

"Don't worry about it," the taller of the two men said, "this was nothing, and we're glad we were able to help. But," he added, shaking a finger with mock seriousness, "next time you move, make sure you line up workers in advance. You can't always count on finding a team just when you need one."

Gwen grinned and assured them she'd learned her lesson when it came to unloading.

Several days later Gwen emerged from her apartment with a satisfied expression on her face. The trailer had been returned; all the boxes had been emptied, broken down and placed in her storage locker; her clothes were unpacked and the kitchen almost felt like it was ready to use. The time had come to take a break and go shopping.

As she walked into the furniture store, Gwen mentally reviewed her budget. She had talked to her accountant the day before and had a good idea of what could safely be spent on furniture for her living room. The entire process made her a little nervous, but very excited. She'd never bought new furniture before. Every-thing she and Emily had used in their Boulder apartment had been second hand — garage sale finds or loans from family members. This was a completely new experience.

Gwen wandered through the showroom with apparent aimless-ness, getting a feel for the store, and what the place had to offer. Her fingers drifted across the smooth grain of a leather sofa. The sales clerks recognized the idle curiosity of the non-buyer and merely smiled at Gwen as she ambled by.

The arbitrary divisions of the store's pseudo-rooms were almost a maze. Gwen wondered if they had consciously been designed on a Celtic knot, like those meditation mazes in France.

Not likely, she thought, smiling to herself. *They're just set up to show off the pieces' possibilities... at least in the hands of a professional decorator.*

Her unstructured wandering halted when she reached the busi-ness office at the center of the store and spied a familiar young woman. Staff moved around the open office with determined precision, accessing computers and plucking pages from whirring printers, but Gwen's attention was focused on one young woman as she approached a distinguished looking older man at the very center of the activity.

It couldn't be... but the young woman turned giving Gwen a full view of her face. What were the odds? Astronomical at best.

"Rachel?" Gwen cried, and launched herself toward the young woman. "Rachel Carson?"

Glancing up, the pretty blonde scanned the showroom for the person who had called her name. When her gaze found Gwen, she hesitated for an instant and then her lips formed a soft "O" of surprise. Her eyes widened and with the swiftness of thought, the color drained from her face and her knees buckled.

The man beside her reacted with startling rapidity. Taking her firmly in his arms, he half-carried, half-led her to a chair, settled her into it and forced her head between her knees. Only then did he glance up to find the source of the blonde woman's distress.

"Mr. Carson," Gwen said as she came to a stop by Rachel's chair. "Is Rachel okay?"

Mr. Carson stared at Gwen with a bemused expression. "She was fine until you called to her," he said, slightly belligerent. "I'm sorry, but do we know you, young lady?"

Gwen, busy examining Rachel's aura to determine if she was in any true danger, almost missed the question. She glanced up quickly. "I'm sorry, sir. It *has* been a long time, I'm not surprised you don't recognize me — I don't look much like I did at twelve."

Mr. Carson stared her in bemusement.

"It's Gwen, Dad." Rachel's whisper was hoarse and strained. She sat up, pushing away his restraining hand. "That's right, isn't it?" Her gaze probed Gwen's eyes. "You're Gwen Vaughan... my best friend from childhood... who died ten years ago." Her voice, calm at first, took on an almost hysterical quality as she choked out the last few words.

Gwen's own knees threatened to give way as she realized what had happened. Glancing wildly around for a chair, she was relieved to see that Mr. Carson was already positioning one directly behind her. She gave him a wan smile and sat without hesitation. Her thoughts ran furiously around her mind as Rachel and her father stared at her in mute accusation.

Right.

Dylan made everyone believe she died with her parents. She was the last person on earth Rachel would expect to see walking around her family's furniture store. She shouldn't have come anywhere near this store.

But... Rachel!

Her best friend from childhood, all grown up. She would've known her anywhere.

What could she say? How could she possibly explain what had happened all those years ago?

At last Gwen opened her mouth, but nothing came out. She licked her dry lips, closed her eyes to gather her strength and tried again.

"I'm sorry I startled you," she said, opening her eyes, and gazing beseechingly at Rachel. "I promise, I'm not a ghost." The forced lightness in her voice failed to relieve the tension in their faces. "I was sent to live with family friends in Colorado. I've only been back in Portland about a week. I'm sorry." She stumbled to a halt. "I'll just go now."

Climbing wearily to her feet, Gwen turned to leave the office when Rachel's voice stopped her.

"If you think you can come in here, announce your resurrection, and then just leave... well, you're a bigger idiot than you were when you were twelve."

Gwen turned in time to see a radiant smile bloom across Rachel's features. Without another word, the pretty blonde wrapped Gwen in an astonishingly fierce hug. "Welcome home, Gwen," she whispered intensely. "I've missed you so much."

Mr. Carson fidgeted with embarrassment, while the two young women dissolved in tears.

"I can see you're going to be of no use the rest of the day," Mr. Carson said to Rachel. "Take the afternoon off. Show Gwen your apartment. You two need some time to catch up."

"Thanks, Dad," Rachel replied, grabbing her purse and practically dragging Gwen to the door.

CHAPTER 22

*R*achel's studio apartment was about six blocks from the big downtown furniture store. The young women walked the short distance, enjoying the calming effect of the exercise. By unspoken consent, they didn't discuss their mutual shock, preferring to wait until they were safely sheltered in Rachel's home.

The apartment was tiny, but Rachel had managed to make it feel snug and secure rather than cramped. The sofa was actually a cleverly disguised daybed. The compact kitchen was neat as a pin, and the breakfast nook served double duty as an office, the secretarial chair rotating efficiently between the built-in computer desk and the little wrought iron café table. Gwen wondered idly if Rachel had done her own interior design. If so, she was definitely going to turn her friend loose on her own sparsely furnished domicile.

"I still can't believe you're here... that you're alive." Rachel shook her head in amazement.

While she studied her friend's living quarters, Gwen's mind raced. What could she say to Rachel? How much could she afford to tell her?

Think, she told herself severely. *If I had run into Rachel before I met Dylan, before I learned the truth about myself, she'd still have had the same questions. What would I have said if I'd run into her before Christmas?*

That line of reasoning calmed Gwen immensely. She didn't have to lie to Rachel. She just had to remember who she was before she learned about being an *Old One.*

"I'm so sorry I upset you, Rachel. I was just so excited to see you." Gwen's eyes were bright, honesty glowing from their depths. "It never occurred to me that you thought I was dead."

"So what, exactly, happened to you?" Rachel asked, then added hurriedly, "If you don't mind talking about it, that is."

Gwen smiled at her friend's sweetness. "It's not a fresh wound, Rachel. I can tell you what I know." For the next hour or so, Gwen and Rachel caught up with each other's lives.

Rachel had led a perfectly normal life, complete with all the teen-age traumas that everyone endures. She had gone to the University of Oregon in Eugene and had studied interior design. As an only child, her father had hoped that she would be interested in the family business, and his desires had been granted. Rachel loved the entire field of interior decoration and even had dreams of expanding the furniture store to include designer paints and flooring. However, at the moment she was in the process of learning the business from the ground up.

Her father had wisely assigned her to be an assistant to the book-keeper for the summer. He understood that unless she knew how the financial end of the business worked, she would be in danger of losing everything when she finally took over on her own.

"So, is there any special guy in your life?" Rachel's eyes gleamed as she broached the subject of romance. "Now don't clam up on me. We've missed ten years of secrets. We've got to get the ball rolling again."

Gwen hesitated, her friend had no idea how many secrets she had. She bit her lip, then decided to dive right in. "Well, there is this one guy... he's a lot older than me, but he's really cute, and I like him a lot."

"Ooo, that sounds promising. Is he back in Colorado? Do you think you'll see him again soon?"

"Actually, he's in California. I'm not sure when I'll see him again, but I'm pretty sure he'll pop into my life again before too long." She grinned, then nudged Rachel with her elbow. "Now, what about you? Did you find the man of your dreams in Eugene?"

"Man of my dreams? In Eugene?" Rachel giggled with at the notion. "Not hardly. Of course I dated some while I was in school, but there was never anyone I was even remotely serious about." She paused, then sighed as her thoughts melted into dreams. "No, I'm still waiting for my knight in shining armor."

"Oh, Rachel," Gwen exclaimed, "this is so wonderful. I've found my best friend again, and we even live close together. Promise me we'll do lots of stuff together and make up for all the years we lost."

Tears glistened in Rachel's eyes as she reached out to hug Gwen. "Absolutely. I'm not letting you get away from me again." A sound like a combined laugh and sob escaped her lips. "You'll think I'm your long lost twin." She released Gwen, grabbed a tissue and wiped her eyes. "Now, when do I get to see this apartment that I'm going to transform into a proper home for you?"

Gwen cleared her throat, discomfort plain on her face. "Rachel, I don't think I can afford to have you work on my apartment."

"Don't be silly." Rachel laughed, the sound ringing gaily around the tiny apartment. "I'll give you my special *my best friend's just returned from the grave* discount." Watching the emotional battle on her friend's face she hurried to add, "Honestly, Gwen, you'd be doing me a favor. Bookkeeping is not my favorite thing, and Dad's not letting me do any design work at the moment. I'm just itching to get my hands on something I can decorate."

Recognizing the pent up frustration of an artist not allowed to create, Gwen relented. "Well, if you're sure... I don't want to start our friendship by taking advantage of you, but I'd love your help."

Rachel clapped her hands with glee. "Wonderful. Now that your conscience is appeased, I repeat: when do I get to see your apartment?"

"How about right now?" Gwen eyed Rachel with speculation. "Is there a sandwich shop or deli between here and there? We could grab some lunch and take it back to my place to eat. That way I won't starve while you're in your creative phase. There's sure not much in my refrigerator at the moment."

Laughing with sheer delight over having found each other again, the young women went out in search of food.

CHAPTER 23

The man watched in fascination as the lovely young woman approached. She was exquisite. Jet black hair framed a perfectly oval face. Her complexion was flawless, a sublime blend of peaches and cream. Her eyes mesmerized him… deep blue pools of inviting warmth.

Her lips curved into a shy smile, and he felt as though he'd been hit in the chest with a sledge hammer.

His senses reeled under an onslaught of full-blown lust. Nothing on this earth would satisfy him but to hold that slender body in his arms… to drown in those beguiling blue eyes… to know they looked only at him. He desperately needed to taste what lay behind those perfect lips, to prove his masculinity by burying himself in her delicious femininity.

He could conquer the world if she was his.

She must be his.

She was designed to be his… and his alone.

Shaking his head, he forced himself to turn away from the vision who stood across the room. His heart beat too rapidly. His palms were glazed with sweat. Glancing down, he was appalled to see that the smooth line of his trousers was marred by an obvious bulge. Quickly he found a chair and folded himself into it, carefully arranging his legs for optimum camouflage.

What's wrong with me? he wondered, his thoughts tinged with desperation. *You'd think I'd never seen a pretty girl before.*

But he knew it was more than that.

This wasn't just a pretty girl.

This was a goddess.

Pull yourself together, man. You see pretty young things every day. You're a university professor, for heaven's sake. You've got a doctorate in anthropology... you're a cultured, civilized man.

But he didn't feel civilized. Not with primal urges burning his blood. He buried his head in his hands and massaged his scalp.

I can't go around thinking about ravaging lovely young women. What if she turns out to be one of my students? Dear God! Don't let her be one of my students...

...to hell with being civilized!

I'm going to have her.

I've got to have her...

NOW.

He glanced up… and started violently.

She was watching him. For an instant he thought he saw a calculating expression in those innocent blue eyes, but it was gone before he could consider its meaning.

He fell completely under the spell spun by her beauty and purity... and spiraled out of control so quickly, so passionately, that he never realized his danger.

Jason Whittier, professor of anthropology at Portland State University, was completely and irrevocably beyond salvation before Lilith even spoke a word.

CHAPTER 24

The morning of June 21st dawned clear and bright, which wasn't always a given in Oregon's Willamette Valley. Gwen stretched and looked down on the park from her third story window.

Today was the day.

Summer Solstice; Midsummer's Day; Alban Heruin.

Whatever it was called, it was a day of unusual power, a day when great magic could occur... especially for the Light.

The equinoxes were days of perfect balance — night and day, Light and Dark, in exact proportion to one another. The solstices were another matter entirely. Today would be the longest day of the year, the twenty-four-hour period with the most hours of light.

It also occurred in the Light half of the year.

The *Old One* calendar divided the year into Light and Dark. Beltane marked the beginning of the period of Light, which coincided fairly well with Spring and Summer; while Samhain began the Dark half, the steadily decreasing light of Fall and Winter.

So... today was an auspicious day for workers of the Light. Today the strands of magic would be especially amenable to Gwen's touch, and today she would seek her third sign. She seriously doubted that Lilith would make any attempt to cross her today. The dictates of power were simply not conducive to Lilith's cause. Gwen smiled in satisfaction as she watched the early morning light brighten to highlight the green velvet of the park.

Padding silently across the soft, rose-brown carpet, Gwen paused before the neat little writing desk that Rachel had insisted was perfect for this corner of the room. Her eyes lit as she remembered the fun she and Rachel had enjoyed as they decorated this room.

Gwen sat down at the desk and reached for the river rock that rested patiently in the drawer. Feeling its smooth, hard weight in the palm of her hand, she reflected on the arbitrary nature of her power. This stone lay in her hand because it had called to her, and her power shown her to its hiding place.

A week ago, she and Rachel had been having lunch in a little café near the river. As it was a warm, sunny day, they had opted to sit on the patio where they could watch the hustle and bustle of the lunchtime pedestrian traffic. Without warning, Gwen's power had kicked in — the first time it had come unbidden since its awakening on her birthday. Startled, she had pretended to study the menu while she followed the golden glow to its destination. Fortunately, the object she needed to find was nearby, and the vision had lasted only a few seconds. Rachel, studying her own menu, had been oblivious to her friend's sudden abstraction.

When they finished their lunch, Gwen had insisted that they take a walk down to Waterfront Park and stroll along the Willamette

River for a few minutes. Rachel had been surprised by the suggestion, but hadn't voiced any opposition. The young women had walked casually, with seeming aimlessness, straight to the place the vision had revealed. There, Gwen had taken off her shoes, stepped into the water, and bent to pick up an ordinary looking river rock.

Returning to her astonished friend, Gwen had simply remarked, "I wanted a souvenir of the Willamette."

Rachel, closing her gaping mouth with a snap, had glanced at the stone and said, "Remind me to keep you away from the Columbia." They had laughed at Gwen's whim and Rachel had returned to work.

Gwen brushed her memories aside with a wave of her hand and turned the stone over to examine its other side. Today a Celtic knot glowed on its surface. She had known immediately that the sigil was there, but its power had been latent, unable to coalesce into being until its appointed time. Today, Alban Heruin, the Light of the Shore, was its moment.

Pulling a piece of paper from the drawer and readying a pen to copy the verse she was sure was about to be revealed, Gwen took a steadying breath and touched the sigil.

Instantly words flowed into her brain with the inexorable current of the river from which the rock had come. She hurried to write them down lest she miss a nuance in their meaning.

> When fire, wind, and earth all encircle your wrist,
> Water too shall come, your sigil to assist.
> Wind is evanescent; it must stand alone.
> The other three must double, High Magic to atone.
>
> The Light of the Shore is the day of longest light.

The Earth is the element you'll need to join your
  fight.
Find me where Atlantic and Mediterranean kiss.
I wait upon The Rock; Africa and Europe bear
  witness.

Gwen stared at the words she had written.

Interesting. The first stanza was about the quest as a whole, not
today's task. So, all four elements would be represented in the
final sigil. She frowned slightly, considering the implications of
the words in front of her. There would be seven signs when the
quest was finished. They'd fit together to make one sigil, and
according to this verse, she'd find two signs relating to fire,
water, and earth, but there would only be one representative of
wind. And she'd already found that one.

Fascinating.

She left her thoughts about the quest as a whole to simmer in her
subconscious as her eyes moved to the second stanza of the verse.

All right. Now she was getting somewhere.

Today was the day... she already knew that.

This sign would be an earth symbol... rock, dirt, metal. Something of that sort.

Where the Atlantic meets the Mediterranean. That was nice and
specific. On a rock... but "rock" was capitalized.

"The Rock." Obviously that was significant.

A place where Europe and Africa were both nearby.

"What is the name of that strait?" she mumbled aloud and stood
to search her bookshelves for her copy of the world atlas. Finding
the oversized book on the lowest shelf, she pulled it out and

thumbed through the pages until she found the map that high-lighted the area of the world surrounding the Mediterranean Sea. Her finger traced the outline of Spain until she reached the Strait of Gibraltar.

She closed her eyes and breathed a sigh of relief.

Of course. The Rock of Gibraltar. That was where her next seeking would take her.

Feeling relaxed and at peace, she allowed herself to rest for a few moments. Gwen was just about to tackle the problem of exactly which moment of this auspicious day would be the most advantageous for her quest when she became aware of a soft, but insistent tapping at the fringe of her consciousness. By allowing her concentration to rest upon it for a moment, she became aware that Mei was waiting to mindspeak her.

Thank you for your attention, Guinevere. The sweetness of Mei's spirit resonated in her mind, leaving a calm assurance in its wake. *I wondered if you would require my assistance today?*

Gwen smiled to herself as she replied, *Thanks for the offer, but today I know what I'm seeking and where to look.*

She allowed the information she had just assimilated to float to the surface of her mind so Mei could read it.

I'm not anticipating any interference from the Dark on this particular power day. What do you think? Am I being overconfident?

Mei hesitated a moment as she considered the data. *No, your reasoning is sound. I don't believe you'll need my support today.* Mei paused briefly, then made her decision. *I'll leave you to your quest. However, I shall remain alert. If you call me, I'll come immediately.*

Thank you, Mei. Gwen was relieved to have her own thoughts confirmed by a more experienced *Old One. I truly hope I don't need your help.*

Blessings upon you, little sister. Mei's calm thought was a benediction; then her presence was gone.

Gwen sighed. She liked Mei, and it was comforting to be part of the larger *Old One* community. However, having someone speak directly into her mind was still a new and distinctly disquieting sensation. She knew the other *Old One*s couldn't actually read her mind — they only had access to what she chose to show them — but she was still uncomfortable with an alien touch inside her own mind. She sighed again and returned to the question of when to initiate her search.

Think... what was the unique feature of this day? The most hours of light...

Okay, what would allow her the maximum use of her advantage, today? When would the light be strongest?

Was that even a valid question?

Normally, she'd choose twilight because of its threshold status. The "not-day-not-night" quality was very conducive to magic.

But that didn't feel like the right answer today.

Standing, Gwen walked back to the window. The sunlight filtering through the trees and falling on the flowers below soothed her soul. She loved the way certain of the flowers seemed to track the sun's progress with their little faces. Right now they were looking east, but at noon they would be oriented straight up, and would seem to be looking right at her.

Of course!

Noon.

That would be the moment to seek the sign: when the sun stood directly overhead.

Throwing her arms wide, Gwen twirled in place, hugging herself in delight. She was absolutely positive that noon was the correct moment, and in her excitement at coming to that conclusion without help, she cried out, "Oh, Renzo!"

Yes, Gwen? His reply was quiet, but firm, echoing deliberately in her mind.

Instantly she stilled and became sober, the thrill of the moment popping like a pricked balloon, shriveling to a hard little knot in the pit of her stomach.

Gwen? Is anything wrong? Renzo's mind-voice took on an edge of panic as she kept her mind tightly closed to the questing tendrils of his thought.

Keeping the shock that she had called him under tight control, Gwen answered him calmly. *Renzo, I'm so sorry. I didn't mean to call you. I'm still a bit clumsy with this mindspeech stuff.*

The warmth of his relief washed through her mind.

Not a problem. I wanted to check in with you today anyway. Would you mind if I came by physically?

You mean teleport here? Now? Panic seized her; she controlled her thoughts rigidly until she could respond calmly. *I'd love to see you, Renzo, but give me a few minutes. I'm not dressed for company.*

She felt him tighten the beam of his thought so that no trace of emotion spilled through his reply. *I'll drop by in about a half-hour, and I'll come the normal way... by the front door.*

Gwen relaxed and exhaled the breath she hadn't realized she'd been holding. Still a bit shaken that she'd called Renzo by accident, she decided she would have to check in with Dylan and learn all she could about mindspeaking. Accidents like the one she'd just had were not to be tolerated, but she wasn't about to ask Renzo for advice on remedying the situation!

Panic surged again, and this time she allowed herself to feel it. Renzo was coming here. To her apartment. They'd be alone… in her private space…

What had she been thinking?

She should have insisted they meet somewhere neutral. A park. A restaurant.

Anywhere but here!

Her hormones ran wild. One moment she felt light-headed and a little nauseous; the next she manic energy flooded her entire body, excitement sizzling in every drop of blood.

She laughed, a bit giddily, to be sure, and let the excitement fuel her race to choose a becoming outfit, dress, and put the apartment to rights.

Everything had to be perfect when he arrived!

CHAPTER 25

*R*enzo stood at Gwen's door at the appointed time. Straightening his shoulders and inhaling deeply, he knocked... and felt like he'd been gut-punched when she opened the door.

He'd always considered the phrase 'she took his breath away' some guy's lame attempt to flatter a girl.

Now he understood that, with the right woman, it could be a statement of literal truth.

He wanted to gasp like a dying fish, but needed to appear cool, calm, and collected, so he smiled and sipped air in short, shallow breaths until his lungs allowed him to breath normally again.

Gwen was beyond beautiful, standing there in tight black jeans that showed off her assets so perfectly when she turned to usher him into her living room. The loose peasant top wasn't bad either, though the string-tie at the neck made him wonder if the pretty little bow might be functional?

He was old enough to remember a time when a simple pull on that ribbon would have loosened the garment, allowing it to fall completely off her shoulders and expose...

He pulled his gaze up to her face... and fell under the spell of those enchanting lips.

His reason kicked in just long enough to realize she'd asked him a question. He searched his memory, but couldn't find the sense of the words those luscious, pink lips had uttered.

"I'm sorry," he said, fighting back an embarrassed flush. "My mind was elsewhere." Nope, he wasn't going to think about exactly *where* his mind had been. "What did you say?"

She laughed. Almost a nervous giggle. He frowned and studied her face. She couldn't be as off-balance as he was... could she?

"I asked if you'd like a cup of coffee?"

He smiled when she caught her pretty lower lip between her perfect white teeth, her gaze flitting sideways.

She was! She was almost as flustered as he was.

"I'd love some coffee."

"Make yourself at home," she said. "I'll be right back."

Relieved to have a moment to regroup, Renzo chose a seat on the red, green, and blue plaid couch, forcing himself to take note of the room. Anything to get his heart rate and breathing under control. Rose-brown carpet. Comfortable looking chintz armchair upholstered in a watery floral pattern that blended nicely with the plaid couch. A writing desk in the corner between the windows, and a nice view of the park.

He felt almost normal by the time Gwen reentered the room and handed him a white ceramic mug of strong, black coffee. The rich fragrance completed his return to sanity, and he smiled and thanked her without difficulty.

"You do take it black, don't you?" she asked, hovering nearby. "I have cream and sugar, if you prefer."

"This is perfect," he said. "Aren't you having any?"

She shook her head, her shoulder-length dark hair glistening in the light from the window. "I've already had a cup, and if I drink too much, I'll be too wired to think straight."

She curled into the chintz armchair and launched into a detailed account of her thoughts on the day's quest. "So," she finished with a rush, "do you think I'm right? Does noon sound like the appropriate time to do this?"

"Uhm, yes... noon sounds right," he said, forcing his gaze away from her beguiling face. "I think I'll hang around 'til you get this done. Is that okay with you?"

Not that he cared whether or not she consented. He wasn't going anywhere until today's task was complete.

He'd spoken with Dylan about the incident on Mt. Everest, and knew that Gwen hadn't intentionally compelled him to stay on the sidelines. Like Dylan, he was confused about what had happened that day. He was aware that Gwen was more powerful than she realized, that she probably didn't need his protection.

But that was just too damn bad, because he intended to protect her anyway.

Ye gods! She was so beautiful. How had he managed to stay away from her for nearly two months?

No matter. He was here now and he wasn't going anywhere. Not until she'd retrieved the sign and was safely home again.

He focused in on her words again in time to hear her say, " ... fabulous. After we finish with the quest stuff, maybe we can have lunch with Rachel. I'd love for you to meet her. She was my best friend when we were kids, and now we've found each other again."

"Great." Renzo loved the idea of spending more time with Gwen, even if he did have to share her with some unknown mortal girl. "We've got a couple hours before noon. Why don't we take a walk? That park down there looks nice."

"Sure. I can show you around campus. Classes start on Monday, so I'll really know my way around the next time you come."

Renzo smiled. He liked the way she assumed he'd be back.

A few minutes before noon they were back in Gwen's living room, their walk around campus a happy memory. As Gwen prepared to search for the third sign, Renzo found himself in a power struggle with her.

"I don't want to argue, Guinevere." He tried to sound calm. He really did, but even he could hear the menace bristling in his voice. "I'm going to keep a light touch on your thoughts and follow you. Dylan did it at Alban Eiler, so you know it's no big deal."

"Of course, it's no big deal." Gwen's voice snapped with irritation. "It's also not necessary. Dylan followed me at Alban Eiler because we had no clue what was going to happen." She paused to catch her breath and glared at him. "I can handle this. I don't need a baby-sitter."

"Well that's just fine," he said, jaw clenching in anger, "because I'm not a baby-sitter. I'm over six hundred years old, and used to getting my own way. So stop whining and get on with it."

Gwen opened her mouth to protest again, but he shouted her down with a glare. "I'm coming, and that's final."

Suddenly Gwen dissolved in giggles, losing her balance and falling into the chintz armchair.

"You think this is funny?" he asked, annoyed at her failure to appreciate the seriousness of the situation.

Her giggles hiccoughed to a stop and she wiped her eyes with the back of her hand. "Actually, yes," she said, trying to stifle another attack of laughter. "We're acting like a couple of six-year-olds trying to out-scream each other."

Renzo watched her with irritation. He wasn't accustomed to being laughed at. But between her hysterical fit of giggles and her explanation, he gave in and grinned with her.

"Okay," she gasped, grabbing a tissue and wiping her still streaming eyes, "you win. Tag along if you must." She took a deep breath, held it for a moment, then let it out with a final little hiccough of laughter. "I think my pride can stand your presence."

"Thank you, Lady Guinevere." Renzo executed a formal bow, ending with an extra flourish. "I feel much better now," he said, eyes twinkling.

"Oh, nonsense," she said. "Let's get this show on the road before we lose our opportunity."

CHAPTER 26

*G*wen adjusted her seat in the chintz armchair, while Renzo prowled the room behind her. Glancing out the window, she saw that the sun had reached its zenith. The time to search had come.

Closing her eyes, she concentrated on the Light of the Shore: a time; but also a place — a sun-warmed beach on the Rock of Gibraltar, where the warm Mediterranean waters kissed the cool of the Atlantic's deep flow.

Gwen entered the gelatinous bubble gently this time — like stepping from her living room onto the balcony outside. No jolting, no jarring. She simply moved to a place where matter fell away from the object of her search. Her power took her swiftly, inexorably east, but she floated gently along its current. She was unaware that she'd resisted the flow of her power before, but this was almost relaxing. She felt Renzo's feather-light touch at the very edge of her mind and accepted its rightness; his presence belonged there.

⌒

RENZO MARVELED at the smooth transition Gwen made from sitting to seeking. He had followed her in the process at Beltane, so he was aware of the differences this time. She was definitely growing into her power. He detected no nervous agitation this time, just focused energy. Until...

His attention shifted rapidly from observing Gwen's search to actively following as she teleported to a beach on the Rock of Gibraltar.

He coalesced beside her and scanned the area for any sign of danger. They stood on a tiny beach nestled between splayed fingers of rock. At the V between the fingers was the black opening of a sea cave. He hurried to catch up as Gwen strode confidently toward the cave. She stopped just inside the mouth of the cave and he watched with an interesting blend of curiosity and excitement as she stretched out her hand toward the lime-stone wall of the cave and touched a particular spot.

A place identical to every other portion of the cave wall to Renzo's eyes, but which came alive at Gwen's touch. He inhaled sharply as a sigil suddenly glowed to life — golden yellow against the moss encrusted darkness of the remainder of the rock. Gently, she plucked the sign from its resting place in the lime-stone bed. She stared at it for a moment, as if memorizing its form, and then turned to share the moment with Renzo.

"See," she whispered, "this was an easy one."

Her face glowed as he took the sign from her fingers and care-fully examined it. Having returned to its native state, the sign was no longer golden. Now the sigil was a cool gray; a sign cut from the living stone of the Rock of Gibraltar. Not smoothly polished, but retaining its natural roughness.

Quietly, Gwen took the sign back from him, held it near the bracelet on her wrist, and watched as it dwindled in size and attached itself to an empty link.

Without warning, their quiet contemplation was interrupted by a raging wind that howled between the outstretched fingers of rock and ripped through the shallow sea cave.

Gwen's hair lashed across her face, and she attempted to capture the dark brown locks in a restraining hand. As she fought the wayward strands, she turned away from the cave, toward the open sea.

She froze, and Renzo turned to see what had immobilized her.

THOUGH SHE GAZED at the place where the open ocean should be, Gwen saw no sky, no waves, no horizon line. Her vision was completely blocked by a massive wall of water. For a moment the wall appeared to hang suspended, both created and arrested by the unnaturally fierce wind.

Then the illusion of timelessness passed.

The wall raced forward, and Gwen realized she was facing her death. Her eyes widened in fear and the blood drained from her face, retreating to her core. Her mind struggled to comprehend what was about to happen.

Renzo turned to see the towering water at the same instant Gwen did. Fortunately, he was far more experienced in reacting to danger than she was. He called her name, and, when she didn't react, pulled her into his arms and teleported without a second's hesitation.

As soon as they materialized in her apartment Renzo forced her limp body into a chair and pushed her head between her knees. "Breathe, Gwen," he said, his voice calm, "you're safe now. Just breathe deeply. You'll feel better in a minute."

He kept up a constant drone of soothing platitudes. She couldn't grasp his words' meaning, but the sound of his voice calmed her, comforted her.

At last, her breathing settled into a normal rhythm and she made an effort to sit up. He removed his hand from the back of her neck where he had been massaging taut muscles as he spoke.

"I'm sorry, Renzo." Tears swam in her eyes, her voice a hoarse whisper. "I feel like such a fool. I was so sure I was ready to handle anything." Gwen stopped abruptly, bit her lip, then blurted out the horrible words. "I'd be dead right now if you hadn't been with me." She burst into tears and drew herself into a ball in the chair.

Renzo knelt in front of her and stroked her back as he continued to murmur in a soothing voice, "You would have been fine, Gwen. You're an *Old One*."

She raised a tear-stained face and wailed, "I didn't even remember that I could teleport. I couldn't think of anything except that I was going to die."

She curled into a tight ball, sobbing convulsively.

CHAPTER 27

*R*enzo's heart ached with Gwen's distress. Unable to stand by and do nothing, he gathered her gently into his arms and slid into the overstuffed chintz armchair beneath her.

She responded by burying her face against his chest and crying even harder.

He held her securely in his arms. He didn't try to soothe or calm her; he simply waited out the storm. At length her breathing eased and her body relaxed; she'd cried herself out.

Handing her the handkerchief he always carried, she dutifully wiped her face and blew her nose before trying to speak.

"Thank you for saving my life," she said quietly. "I've made a mess of your shirt." She made a wry face as she touched the spot where her tears had soaked the fabric.

"It'll dry," he replied brusquely, "and you're welcome. I'm just glad I was there."

Gwen nestled closer into his encircling arms. The emotional storm had left her drowsy and lethargic. She knew she should get up and try to explain herself, but she was too drained to think straight. She was warm... and dry... and safer than she'd ever felt in her life... she'd get up in a bit...

It took Renzo a minute to realize that she'd fallen asleep in his arms. He hugged her a little tighter and thought ruefully that his legs might be asleep as well before long. But, it didn't matter. Nothing mattered save that she was alive and safe.

If she'd cried herself to sleep, he wasn't about to wake her. He settled himself as comfortably as he could in the big overstuffed chair and prepared to lapse into a light doze himself.

He woke to find his lap empty. He fought a wave of panic and forced himself to extend his senses in search of her. Immediately, he heard her humming quietly to herself in the kitchen. Relaxing, he recognized the enticing aroma of frying bacon.

He stood, stretched and went in search of the bathroom. When he made his way to the kitchen a few minutes later, he found Gwen calmly assembling bacon, lettuce and tomato sandwiches.

Seeing him standing in the doorway, she smiled. "We missed lunch with Rachel. I called her to apologize a little bit ago. She was only slightly miffed, and insisted that we have dinner with her tonight. I figured a couple of BLTs would hold us 'til then."

He leaned against the door jamb and watched her quick, efficient movements as she put the light meal together. He couldn't understand why the most mundane activities suddenly became fascinating when Gwen performed them. Scrubbing his hand across his face, he wondered if some of her magic was in the realm of the siren?

That was patently ridiculous, of course. Dylan hadn't had any trouble seeing her as just another young *Old One* to be guided along the path of Light.

Obviously, he wasn't Dylan.

Gwen definitely wasn't just another *Old One* to Renzo. But, maybe she should be. Maybe his fascination with her was a problem; maybe he should remove himself from her life.

Perhaps he should speak to Merlin?

Then again, maybe he shouldn't.

A flash of anger heated his blood at the thought that if he hadn't insisted on accompanying her, Gwen would be dead.

Mei hadn't insisted on tagging along.

Dylan would have let her go alone.

Even as he'd argued with her, Renzo had been all too aware that every other *Old One* would have agreed that it was her right to pursue her quest as she saw fit.

Yet his fascination with her had saved her life.

"Renzo? Are you all right?"

He startled, surfacing from his reverie to find Gwen standing in front of him, a worried expression on her face.

"Sorry. I was lost in thought. What did you say?"

She smiled and touched his arm. "Lunch is ready. Come sit down."

They talked about inconsequential things while they ate. When they finished, Gwen took his hand and met his gaze with serious eyes.

"Thank you again, Renzo. For everything. Not only did you save my life, but you also handled my hysterical reaction perfectly. I'm very lucky to have you as a friend."

He glanced away, embarrassed. "Like I said, I'm just glad I won the fight so I was there."

Her cheeks flushed a very attractive pink. "Yes. Well, about that," she said, speaking quietly and rapidly, "you were right. I did need help. I mean, what kind of an *Old One* forgets she has the power to teleport when she's in a life-threatening situation?" She bit her lip and stared at the toast crumbs on her now empty plate.

Renzo smiled ruefully. "A very inexperienced *Old One*." He sighed. "Gwen, I'm not quite sure what's going on. I can't think of another *Old One* who has had to deal with life and death situations during his or her initial quest. If you were anyone other than yourself, you wouldn't have needed me there today."

She glanced up sharply, and he watched as comprehension dawned.

"You mean," she said in a tone of surprise, "Lilith doesn't try to kill every new *Old One* during their initiation to power?"

"That's exactly what I mean. This has never happened before. I don't understand what her problem with you is, but she definitely has it in for you... and has since you were a child."

They sat in silence for a moment remembering the car accident that had killed her parents, and would have killed her except for Dylan's intervention.

"She's only attacked me once," Renzo continued, "and that was in order to draw Dylan away from you. No one will ever know how she lured your parents out that night, but if Dylan hadn't been drawn away to protect me, it's likely she wouldn't have been able to pull it off."

He stared into her beautiful gold-tinged brown eyes. "She wants you dead, Gwen. We can't afford to forget that."

"You're thinking she was responsible for that huge wave?" she asked with quiet intensity.

"I'm sure of it," he agreed with a nod. "That was no accident. We didn't just get caught by incoming tide."

"Well, her malicious intent doesn't excuse my stupidity. I mean, I just stood there waiting to be drowned." Gwen shook her head in chagrin. "But it does help to explain why I seem to need a keeper." She gazed at Renzo with a solemn expression. "I'd appreciate it if you'd plan to come with me when I seek the last four signs."

Renzo nodded, equally sober. "You've got a deal."

"Thank you. Again."

Reaching across the table, he took her hand. "Wherever this journey takes us, I'll be right there beside you."

She squeezed his fingers. "I couldn't ask for a better partner."

When the silver chime sounded, they both glanced up, and then stared at each other with matching quizzical expressions.

Gwen broke the surprised silence. "I guess High Magic approves of our decision."

Contentment flooded Renzo's heart as he studied Gwen. She was unlike any other woman he'd ever known. Unexpected and unpredictable.

And she was unutterably, unaccountably perfect for him.

And High Magic knew it… had very likely planned it.

"I'm glad," he said, knowing he'd have risked High Magic's wrath to stay beside this amazing woman. "Whatever the future holds, we'll tackle it as a team."

Together.

Forever, if he had anything to say about it.

And Lorenzo Alan Santini intended to say a lot!

ALSO BY DEBBIE MUMFORD

Kristi Lundrigan Mysteries:

- DELECTABLE MOUNTAIN QUILTING (NOVEL)
- IN A PICKLE (NOVEL)
- FOOL'S PUZZLE (SHORT STORY)
- WILDFIRE! (SHORT STORY)

Gus and Ghost Short Story Series:

- SEVENTH
- SEVENTH: FIRST FRUITS
- DEATH OF AN ALCHEMIST (UNCOLLECTED ANTHOLOGY)
- SEVENTH: THE SAMHAIN DILEMMA
- DARK OF THE MOON (UNCOLLECTED ANTHOLOGY)

Logans of Lastalrig Series:

- HER HIGHLAND LAIRD (NOVELLA)
- HER HIGHLAND YULE (SHORT STORY)

Red's Series:

- RED'S MAGICK (SHORT STORY COLLECTION)
- SEEING RED (SHORT STORY)

Signs of the Prophecy Novels:

- YOUNGEST
- SEEKER

- CHOSEN (COMING SOON!)

Sorcha's Children Series:

- SORCHA'S CHILDREN (OMNIBUS EDITION)
- SORCHA'S HEART (NOVELLA)
- DRAGONS' CHOICE (NOVEL)
- DRAGONS' FLIGHT (NOVEL)
- DRAGONS' DESIRE (NOVEL)
- DRAGONS' DESTINY (NOVEL)

Supernatural Yellowstone Short Story Series:

- REALITY BITES
- THE CAT LADY OF YELLOWSTONE

Uncollected Anthology Short Stories:

- DEATH OF AN ALCHEMIST (UA ALCHEMY)
- THE WEDDING CAKE (UA MAGICAL ARTS)
- DARK OF THE MOON (UA PARANORMAL PIRATES)
- IN THE BANYAN COPSE (UA UNEXPECTED HISTORIES)
- OLD ONE (UA MAGICAL QUESTS)

Universal Star League Short Story Series:

- VOYAGES INTO THE BLACK (COLLECTION)
- THE WARBIRDS OF ABSAROKA
- AWAKENING THE WARRIOR
- INCIDENT ON THE ODYSSEY
- THE QUEEN'S CAPTIVE
- THE LOST COLONY
- FREIGHTER FAMILIES IN SPACE

Witchling Short Story Series:

- WITCHLING
- THE SOLITARY SORCERESS
- TO PROTECT A PRINCESS

Stand Alone Novels:

- SECOND SIGHT

Historical Fiction:

- HER HIGHLAND LAIRD (NOVELLA)
- HER HIGHLAND YULE
- INCIDENT ON THE HIGH LINE
- MISS BAINBRIDGE'S SUMMER ADVENTURE
- MISS BAINBRIDGE'S CHRISTMAS PARTY
- SISTERS IN SUFFRAGE
- THE TRAIL WHERE WE CRIED
- THE WHITE DRAGON AND THE RED

Short Story Collections:

- LOVE IN A FLASH
- TALES OF BYGONE DAYS
- TALES OF LOVE & MAGICK
- TALES OF THE UNEXPECTED
- TALES OF TOMORROW
- TALES OF DISASTROUS DEEDS

Short Fiction:

- A GROVE OF MOUNTAIN ASH
- A WALK WITH GEORGIA

- ASTROMANCER
- BECAUSE OF THE CHRISTMAS STROLL
- BENEATH AND BEYOND
- DEEP DREAMING
- DELIA'S DECISION
- EGG THIEF
- ICE STORM
- INCIDENT ON THE HIGH LINE
- IN SEARCH OF A VALENTINIAN
- MISS BAINBRIDGE'S CHRISTMAS PARTY
- MISS BAINBRIDGE'S SUMMER ADVENTURE
- NEEDLE-GREEN
- NEW YEAR
- OPENING HER EYES
- REMEMBRANCE
- SILVER-TIPPED DEATH
- SIMON SAYS
- SISTERS IN SUFFRAGE
- SKYE DREAMS
- SPINNING
- THE TIE THAT BINDS
- THE TRAIL WHERE WE CRIED
- THE WHITE DRAGON AND THE RED
- TO DREAM OF FLYING
- TREASURES
- TRIAL ON THE TRAIL
- WAKINYAN'S VALLEY

"WDM Presents" Anthologies:

- TALES OF MYSTERY & MAYHEM
- 2016: A YEAR OF SHORT FICTION
- 2017: A YEAR OF SHORT FICTION
- WDM PRESENTS: SHORT FICTION FROM 2018

Want to know what happens next? Here's a sneak peek of *Seeker*, the second book in the *Signs of the Prophecy* series.

Rachel and Gwen strolled casually down the street near Gwen's apartment. It was the Fourth of July, and the two young women had decided to celebrate their freedom with a trip to the Portland Art Museum. Since it was a beautiful summer day and the museum was only a few blocks from Gwen's apartment, they had decided to walk.

"I've always loved these park blocks between the university and the museum," Rachel said as they ambled along enjoying the sunlight filtering through the green of the park's trees. "I'm so glad you chose that apartment. Now I've got an excuse to loiter in the park."

Gwen laughed. "Happy to be of service," she said with a mock bow.

"Here it is." Rachel indicated the massive building across the street from where they stood. Heading to the corner, the young women crossed the street and ascended the broad steps leading up to the main entrance.

As they stood in line to buy their tickets, Gwen noted the combination of cool marble stairs and warm wood parquet floors with approval. *Balance,* she thought, *this place is in balance. No wonder it radiates such a soothing atmosphere for its patrons.*

Gwen and Rachel spent several hours contemplating the various styles of art showcased by the large museum. When their protesting feet and legs finally convinced them they couldn't handle another moment of standing in awed appreciation, they strolled to the elegant little café and collapsed into comfortable chairs.

"I didn't realize you were so taken with Asian art," Gwen exclaimed after ordering a summer salad with shrimp and an iced tea.

"Oh, yes," Rachel breathed, "this whole area is permeated with a strong Asian influence. I'm not sure how you could grow up here and not respond to it. We'll have to visit the Chinese Garden and the Japanese Garden soon. They're so beautiful."

Gwen's mind wandered as her friend rhapsodized on about the wonders of the art and architecture of the Far East. As her mind flitted from thought to thought, she became aware of an intensity of interest that seemed to be directed at herself and Rachel. Her pulse quickened as this awareness claimed center stage in her awareness, and she quickly scanned the room. The café was nearly empty, a fact that had allowed her to notice the scrutiny. She allowed her senses to roam across the little gift shop that sat just beyond the opening to the café.

And found her quarry. A man whose attention was focused on their table.

She glanced quickly back to Rachel in order to avoid making eye contact with him. No need to alert him to the fact that she'd noticed his interest. Making a few affirmative noises for Rachel's benefit, she allowed the surface of her mind to rest lightly on their conversation, while the main part of her awareness remained on their unknown observer.

She searched her memory; she was certain she had seen his face before.

Of course. He had been rearranging a display in the Asian Art exhibit. Fine, he was a museum employee. Was he wearing an identification badge?

Gwen chanced a quick glance in his direction, and confirmed that he was indeed wearing a badge clipped to his suit jacket. Had they done something wrong? Something to suggest they might be art thieves? A chill stole across her soul, and she worked to suppress a shiver of fear as her mind leapt to the next logical conclusion.

Was he under Lilith's influence?

She raised her eyes again and studied his face, her mind running through the sigils that would be most effective in disabling him in such a public place.

Ah-ha, no need. False alarm.

She smiled to herself, allowing her defenses to return to their normal state. The man wasn't interested in Gwen at all. His attention was clearly fixed on Rachel. When she studied him that last time, her concern banished by decision, she'd been able to observe him in more detail. He was clearly focused on the lovely young woman sitting across the table from her.

No longer feeling threatened, Gwen realized she had been stealing glances at him through an exceptionally clear aura. No malice muddied her perceptions of his face and form. The man wasn't a threat, but he was very interested in Rachel.

David moved quietly across the gift shop to get a better view of the two young women in the café. If he was honest with himself, which he always tried to be, he'd have to admit he was only interested in observing the diminutive blonde. He watched in delight as she tossed her head and laughed animatedly, her honey blonde curls shining in the clear sunlight streaming through the large café windows. He hadn't been close enough yet to determine her eye color, but it didn't matter. They were large and intelligent, and sparkled with mischief as she chatted happily with her dark-haired friend.

The young women stood up and prepared to leave. He panicked. He had to meet her. He couldn't just let her walk out of the museum, he might never find her again. What could he say? How could he approach her? He watched as they paid for their lunch, thoughts running furiously through his mind.

They walked toward him. In a moment they would be past him— on their way into the huge city that waited outside the museum's doors. This was it. It was now or never...

Gwen watched the young man surreptitiously as she and Rachel made their way to the front of the gift shop and the waiting museum entrance. She could almost see the panic racing across his expressive face. She hid a smile behind a counterfeit cough as they drew even with him. As she had expected, he stepped into their path, blocking their progress. Rachel stopped and looked up at him, startled by his sudden appearance.

"Excuse me, ladies." His voice sounded slightly strangled, but he cleared his throat and continued. "I couldn't help noticing your interest in the Asian Art exhibit. I wondered if you might like a tour of our acquisitions department?"

Oh, please! Gwen stifled the desire to roll her eyes. *That's got to be the worst pick-up line I've ever heard.*

Rachel frowned at the earnest young man. "A tour of the acquisitions department? Are you for real?"

The young man flushed to the roots of his dark brown hair. "I'm David Milligan, assistant to the curator for the Asian Art department," he said, his voice calming. "If you're interested, I'd be happy to show you around our acquisitions department." As he spoke he escorted them out of the gift shop and into the spacious entrance hall.

"Nice to meet you, David Milligan." Gwen's comment forced the young man to to look away from Rachel and turn his attention to her. "I'm Guinevere Vaughan and this is Rachel Carson. We'd love a behind-the-scenes tour," she smiled as his face lit with relief, "but not today. Shall we call your office for an appointment?"

The smile froze on his face, but he recovered his poise and he reached into his jacket pocket, pulling out a business card. Handing it to Gwen, he nodded.

"That would be fine. Please ask for me by name. Good afternoon, Miss Vaughan, Miss Carson." His gaze lingered on Rachel's face for a moment, then he turned and walked away.

Rachel's eyes followed his progress until he turned a corner. Then she sighed and looked at Gwen. "Was that what I think it was?" she asked with a nervous giggle.

"Shh," Gwen said. "We'll talk when we get outside."

They hurried out the door, down the wide stairs and across the street into the park. Once there, Gwen's control broke and she cried, "Rachel's got a boyfriend," in the sing-song pattern of a ten-year-old.

Rachel promptly responded by hitting her. "And how do you know it's me he was after? You're the one holding his card." But she blushed, looking very pleased.

"Yeah, right, he was so interested in me that he could hardly tear his eyes away from you," Gwen teased, grinning broadly. She handed Rachel his card. "So, are you going to call and make an appointment?"

"Oh, definitely." she said. Her eyes widened and she grasped Gwen's hands. "You'll come with me, won't you?" she asked, the pleading note in her voice unmistakable. "I mean, why did you say we'd make an appointment, anyway?"

"Of course I'll come with you. I wouldn't miss the sequel to this encounter for the world." She expertly dodged the purse Rachel swung at her before continuing. "I said we'd make an appointment so the ball would be in your court. I figured you deserved the chance to decide whether you wanted to follow through without him looming over you."

Rachel's eyes glazed, her expression bemused. "He did kind of tower over me, didn't he? What would you guess? Six foot... maybe six-two?"

"Well, anyone looks tall to you, midget," Gwen chortled.

"I am not a midget. I'm five-two. And very happy with my height, thank you very much." She tried to look annoyed, but failed miserably. They lapsed into silence as Rachel stared dreamily into space.

~

Look for *SEEKER* at your favorite online retailer.

ABOUT DEBBIE MUMFORD

Debbie Mumford specializes in speculative fiction—fantasy, paranormal romance, and science fiction. Author of the popular *Sorcha's Children* series, Debbie loves the unknown, whether it's the lure of space or earthbound mythology. Her work has been published in multiple volumes of *Fiction River*, as well as in *Heart's Kiss Magazine*, *Spinetingler Magazine*, and other popular markets. She writes about dragon-shifters, time-traveling lovers, and ghostly detectives for adults as Debbie Mumford and contemporary fantasy for tweens and young adults as Deb Logan.

Join Debbie's special announcement newsletter list and receive a FREE story!

To learn more, visit Debbie at:
debbiemumford.com/
Or send her an email at:
deborah.mumford@gmail.com

facebook.com/DebbieMumfordWrites
amazon.com/author/debbiemumford
bookbub.com/authors/debbie-mumford
twitter.com/deborah_mumford